LINDA

KINS

FLASH

by the same author

THE RUNNING FOXES

A BREED OF GIANTS

REX

CASEY

RUSTY

ZARA

CHIA, THE WILDCAT

LAKELAND VET

WALK A LONELY ROAD

NEVER COUNT APPLES

NEVER TELL A SECRET

FLASH

Joyce Stranger

COLLINS & HARVILL PRESS
London, 1976

© 1976 Joyce Stranger Limited

ISBN 0 00 261249 6

Set in Monotype Baskerville
Made and printed in Great Britain by
William Collins Sons & Co. Ltd, Glasgow
for Collins, St James's Place and
Harvill Press Ltd, 30A Pavilion Road,
London SW1

To Pat and Ed
with all my love

This book is fiction.
All the people in it are imaginary.

Chapter One

The boy should not have been there, but Andrew Grant hadn't the heart to send him home. They had waited together from milking time; they had watched the stars come out of the dark and the moon rise high; they had sat together in the farm kitchen, watching and hoping, while Megan, the ten-year-old collie, moved her body painfully, waiting for the litter that should never have been conceived.

If only she hadn't got out.

She was far too old for pups and Andrew would never forgive himself.

He bent over her, fondling her head, and she waved her tail gently. She had little time for him. All her feelings were concentrated on the very faint birth pains that had been needling her for the past few hours. She had known five litters, and enjoyed motherhood, but this time there was none of the sudden swift pain, the drive of the pup into the world. Only a growing unease, so that she moved restlessly, circling the room, and panting uncomfortably. Andrew could not bear the sight of her burdened body. He should have had her spayed. He was a fool.

He stood up to brew tea. He was a slender man in his early thirties, a lonely man, left a widower by the death of his young wife in an accident some years before. The loss had bound him to Geordie, who had come to live with his grandmother in the village when his parents both died in a multiple crash on the M1. Geordie still limped from his own injuries. The lame leg was healing but the doctors would not say if it would ever be right.

Andrew pushed his thick dark hair away from his eyes and looked across at the boy. Geordie was small for an eleven-year-old, brown-eyed, brown haired and fair skinned. He would have been a plain child had it not been for those eyes; enormous, expressive, and just now focused on the bitch with such intensity that Andrew began to worry.

He should send the child home.

Suppose the bitch died?

'Home, Geordie, as soon as we have had our tea,' Andrew said.

The brown eyes flashed indignantly.

'You said I could stay. Grandy said I could stay. I've never seen puppies born.'

And I'm not sure you will now, Andrew said, but he said it to himself. Another half hour at most and he would have to ring the vet. The bitch was already overdue and the pups should have begun to come by now. She whimpered, and tore at the newspaper lining her box.

'I think she's going to need help,' Andrew said. 'It should have been over by now. I thought she'd have had them today. It's high time you went home.'

'Grandy's at a meeting, and I don't like being home alone,' Geordie said. He had been longing all week for the puppies, especially when Andrew had said he could stay and watch so long as Megan didn't object to him and warn him away by growling. Geordie was sure she would not. He and the bitch were inseparable when he was at the farm. He stroked the soft white ruff, and the bitch licked his hand.

'She wants me to stay,' Geordie said.

Andrew made the tea and poured it into the two big mugs. Sheena Graham would have been horrified if she had seen how strong it was. Geordie was only allowed milky tea at home. He took it rapturously. Andrew always treated him like an adult, and not like a baby. The boy often felt his grandmother had no idea that he was grown up; she still thought of him as a five-year-old, just starting school, and she hated him running or trying to play games, afraid that he might injure the healing leg. He had spent six months in plaster, and now had to have treatment twice a week in the hospital in Glasgow, which was a long and tiring journey for both of them.

Andrew walked to the window and looked out. Night hid the stone houses that nestled under the mountain. The moon glowed in the waters of the loch; a ruffled globe that shivered and broke and vanished as cloud wisped around it, promising rain.

Andrew looked up.

There was a ring around the moon. Bad weather, and they had had plenty of that recently. Bad for the sheep on the hill, suffering from fluke and footrot, and bad for the few crops he grew, suffering from mould and from wind that flattened them, making harvesting difficult and expensive.

The village of Drumkinnon was patched with light. Light from MacDonald's house beside the garage; light from the ugly hotel on the side of the hill where fishermen congregated and talked of salmon as if nothing else in the world existed; light from the manse, where the Minister laboured over his Sunday sermon; light from the little schoolhouse where Miss MacDougal marked the children's books.

Andrew turned back to the room. Geordie was kneeling beside the bitch, holding her head as she whimpered. Her eyes stared up at her master, agonised, and Andrew cursed to himself softly and ran to the telephone. She was in trouble and he was a purblind idiot and should have recognised the fact long before.

The ringing bell showed no sign of stopping. On and on, into an empty silence. But if Angus McGregor were out, he would have left a recorded message. He must be in.

The bitch whimpered again.

'McGregor here,' a voice said, suddenly, loud and brusque.

'Megan's in trouble,' Andrew said.

'I'm no' surprised. Bring her in and quickly and I'll be ready. Do you think I'll need to operate?'

'I don't know,' Andrew said. 'Geordie's here. I'll drop him on my way.'

'It's out of your way and ye'd best be quick, with the bitch almost eleven,' Angus said. 'Bring the lad and I'll phone Sheena. He'll not hurt. He can wait with my wife; she'll find him something to eat. Boys are always hungry.'

'Can I come?' Georgie asked, and followed Andrew, ecstatic, in spite of a needling worry about the bitch. But Andrew would not let harm come to her, and neither would the vet. Geordie had supreme confidence in both the men. Angus McGregor had operated on an in-lamb ewe last year and saved her life and Geordie had bottle-fed the lamb, a fine young ram now running on the mountain with the rest of the flock, always coming to greet the boy, tame as a dog after hand-rearing.

The stars had gone, hidden by dense cloud. The wind was keen and man and boy shivered as they climbed into the old soft-top Land-Rover. Geordie had christened it Old Badger as its engine snuffled and snarled like the tame badger kept at the garage, and now he willed the cantankerous engine to turn over and cough swiftly into life, instead of spluttering and choking.

His wish worked.

Andrew put the vehicle into gear, and released the hand-brake and they were off, Megan lying in her basket in the back, with Geordie crouched beside her, trying to keep it from bumping too much.

It was a forlorn hope.

The unmade lane from the farm was pocked and rutted and the headlights failed to reveal half the pitfalls. The vehicle crashed into a rut, and heaved itself out again, and the basket slid.

The bitch whined again. Geordie, holding her tightly, could feel shudders under her skin. Her nose was hot and dry, and she was panting so much he was afraid she would

12

burst her lungs.

They turned out of the lane on to the main road. The mountain loomed beside them, black against the grey of night. The headlights flashed across the water of the loch, picking out a small fishing boat, labouring against the wind and the waves; flicking rough water to life with a flash and a gleam; sweeping over a whitewashed two-roomed cottage belonging to Mary McStraten, who was said to be the grand-daughter of a woman burned for witchcraft. Geordie was a little afraid of her, of her bent shape and gnarled face, and toothless half-wit grin. There was a light in her window now, and her shadow was humped and black across the curtain.

A cat fled across the road and vanished in the heather.

Rain drifted down the windscreen and the wipers set up their monotonous rhythm.

Dear God, let Megan be all right. Dear God, let Megan be all right.

The panting was worse, and fear settled on Geordie. He had never felt safe since his parents died. One minute they were all there laughing together and the next . . . Memory returned; the sudden scream of brakes, the crash of metal, and shouts. He gripped the back of Andrew's seat, unable to still the terror that poured over him, so that he was wet with sweat. He had thought that was over and that he was no longer afraid in a car, but now he braked for every corner, willing Andrew to slow down, not wanting to say anything least he were thought to be a baby. He wanted so desperately to help Andrew, to appear adult, to show that he too could farm. When he grew up he was going to Agricultural College. Animals were all that mattered.

Megan whined, high and frighteningly.

'Soothe her, lad,' Andrew said, and put his foot down on the accelerator, so that Geordie felt bile come into his throat and waited with horror for the inevitable thrust of brakes, and the rending cry as the car went out of control.

He swallowed, and looked out of the window. They were passing the hotel; passing the iron jetty where the boats tied up when they came to the village for diesel fuel and for stores; passing the garage, where the big Alsatian followed them with his eyes and speeded them with his barking; past the village shop, where Annie McGrath sold stamps and food and knitting wool and dog biscuits and fishing hooks and outboard engines and paraffin and the home-made cakes that her daughter Nettie, who was not quite right in the head, baked every day. Nettie could cook and sew, but if you spoke to her she looked bright eyed and had nothing to say, or mumbled something that nobody could understand. But she always made a special cake for Geordie, unable to tell him how sorry she was that his parents had died and he had to limp all the time.

Nettie was standing in the doorway watching the night. She waved as they passed, Geordie waved back to her, and returned to his bumpy vigil, crouched on his haunches, steadying the bitch.

They were off the main road, and speeding up the mountain flank, along the twisting narrow road, with Andrew praying they would meet no one as he did not want to have to reverse. It was a crazy short cut to take in the dark, but it saved almost five miles. Angus lived in the next village.

The mountain fell away behind them and the engine growled as they mounted the road. A sheep, sound asleep in the middle of the fairway, ambled off awkwardly on stiff legs and bumbled into the ditch. An owl drifted by, ghostly, and Geordie shivered. Bird of evil, bird of ill omen. Who said that? He couldn't remember. He was always looking for omens; for good signs and bad, catching falling leaves and wishing, wishing on a new moon, touching wood. His mother had been very superstitious. She believed implicitly in horoscopes and always read hers anxiously at the beginning of the day.

Avoid travel, hers had said, that fatal day, last year.

His father had laughed. Geordie hadn't laughed when he woke up in hospital. He had remembered. But Grandy didn't believe in the stars, and tried her best to convince Geordie that nothing could have made any difference to that day. She was intensely religious, and God knew best.

Geordie thought of her now, walking slowly along the road home after a committee meeting of the Ladies of the Village, who planned all the fund raising for various charities. She was the secretary, and spent much of her time writing letters on behalf of the other ladies. They called themselves the Distaff committee, which puzzled Geordie who had never thought to ask his grandmother what it meant. He thought it had something to do with shepherds' staffs; words could be very baffling.

Grandy was small and very old indeed; nearly seventy. She sometimes had blinding headaches, and then Geordie went to see Andrew and spent the day on the farm. He wished he had had a brother or a sister. It was very lonely being an orphan and though Grandy was kind, she tired easily and said 'no' more often than she said 'yes'.

The Land-Rover was running downhill. Andrew kept his foot on the brakes, negotiating the hairpin, his heart briefly lurching as it always did on that corner when the headlights pointed into space. Then they revealed banked heather and another sheep which ambled slowly into cover, momentarily dazzled by the unexpected glare.

Below them was the farm at the end of the corrie. Lights spilt from the doorway into the yard. A dog barked as they passed and chased briefly after them, furious at their intrusion. Megan summoned her energy and barked back, but it was a feeble noise worrying Geordie more than anything else that night. Megan usually repulsed all invaders with full-throated barking.

Then they were on the main road and Andrew was speeding again, the Land-Rover covering the miles until they had left the end of the loch behind and come to the edge of Drumbeattie. They passed the straggle of homes and the tiny fishing hotel and the brash new red brick houses on the little estate where retired Englishmen and their wives found sanctuary after lives spent in crowded cities. The last building was an old house in vast overgrown grounds. The headlights flashed briefly on the sign: Tigh na Bhet.

The vet's house. Geordie expelled a long breath. They were there, they were safe, and Megan would be all right now. She had to be all right. He watched as Andrew lifted the bitch gently in his arms and carried her in through the open door.

At any other time Geordie would have been fascinated all over again by the vet's house. By the immense stone flagged hall, where spears and daggers and duelling pistols hung on the walls and a large bronze statue of Venus was decked with the children's school hats and satchels; by the bronze eagles and deer on the vast hall table; by the stuffed pheasants and ducks in the glass case at the end of the hall by the surgery door; by the tubes on the table containing kidneys and pieces of liver, embryo fish, a tapeworm. Angus McGregor was the bane of his wife, who never quite knew what he would bring home next; an aeroplane propeller, or the engine of a vintage car, or a fishing float washed up on the beach that might come in handy, one never knew.

Annoyingly some of his trophies did come in handy like the Venus which made an exceptionally useful hallstand and was usually well hidden by the family's coats. And the enormous old-fashioned flat-iron that propped open the waiting-room door; and the wicker fish basket that held logs.

A log fire burned now at the end of the hall, the flames casting unlikely shadows. The coated Venus was a bulky monster, dark and brooding against the panelling. There was a movement on the hearthrug. A muddle of furry bodies sorted itself into a tabby cat and two kittens;

16

a sleepy-eyed Labrador pup; Tycho, the fox cub, hissing to himself at the approach of strangers, but held down firmly by Tab, who had adopted him with her kittens. He bit her paw, hating to be held against his will and she slapped him soundly across the face to teach him better manners.

Angus was waiting for them in the doorway of his surgery. He was a bull of a man, broad-shouldered, massive paunched, with the blond hair of a Viking and blond beard to match. His blue eyes were usually merry but just now they were fierce as he looked at the bitch and beckoned Andrew in to the room.

'Can't I come with her?' Geordie asked.

'No, lad. Get to the kitchen and find Donald and Davina. They're making toffee apples for bonfire night. Ye can help them and come over for the fireworks too. Away wi' you.'

The door shut.

Geordie stood looking at it, and wandered over to the fire. He was unaware of anything but a worry that had flared to mask all his thoughts. Supposing Megan died? Andrew had promised him a pup for himself. A collie pup. Megan had mated with Fly, who was one of the best dogs around and whose master won every trial with him. Not that Andrew cared for trial collies. He liked a working animal that could round the sheep on the hill and run a tireless seventy miles a day to its master's twenty.

Tab was washing her kittens. The fox cub had curled up against her for warmth. A local farmer had killed his mother and his litter mates and overlooked him. Tartar, the big Alsatian, had brought the cub home in his mouth, having heard him whimper with cold and hunger. He had been a wee blind rickety thing. He was now sturdy and mischievous, and wicked tempered. He was going to be a major problem too.

There were warm smells coming from the kitchen. Geordie knew his way around the place. It was more like a museum than a house, he thought, stopping to look at two cases filled with bright tropical butterflies, their vivid colours iridescent, glittering in the firelight.

There were deer heads on the walls, and two fox masks, one open mouthed and grinning and the other with the mouth closed, the lips lifted in a permanent snarl. Beyond it was a vast canvas, a Victorian picture in a broad gilt frame, badly in need of dusting. *The Fighting Temeraire.*

Angus, who loved poetry, and the riproar of balladry, and sang old Scottish songs at the top of his considerable voice, had recited the poem to Geordie only the week before. He had followed it up with the tale of the *Revenge*, which Geordie infinitely preferred for its rolling phrases.

> And Sir Richard said again,
>   'We be all good English men,
> Let us bang these dogs of Seville,
>   the children of the devil,
> For I never turned my back
>   upon Don or devil yet.'

It must be exciting to have Angus for a father, Geordie thought, missing his own parents so much that it hurt all over again and he did not want to join the twins in the kitchen. They were as noisy and boisterous as Angus himself. And no one ever quite knew what Donald would do next either. He had spent the summer, unknown to his parents, taking people across the loch in the family rowing boat when the ferryman had decided it was too rough for him to go out. His father did not discover this until the Minister had called, and told how Donald had rowed through the wildest weather of the year; the Minister, who had not realised how rough it was, praying the whole way, and Donald laughing at the wind and pulling on the oars and singing sea shanties.

There was no pocket money for six months for those escapades, and there was a long lecture as well. Now Donald had a scheme for taming a deer, and teaching it to draw a cart. So far, he had been totally unsuccessful. He hadn't even caught a deer. Davina was as bad as her brother. She had fallen down the cliff trying to photograph an osprey's nest. The birds attacked her and she lost the camera as well, but being Davina had fallen on soft earth and climbed back as if nothing had happened.

The twins were both slender, dark haired, like their mother, but with their father's vivid blue eyes and robust temperament. The noise coming from the kitchen now would have made Grandy's head ache for a week.

'Geordie! What are you doing here?'

Geordie thought Catherine McGregor the most beautiful woman he had ever seen. She was tiny, not as tall as he, with a vivid dark-skinned face, and brilliant dark grey eyes. Her cheekbones slanted upwards, and her wide mouth laughed most of the time. She was a memory of the Armada, his grandmother said, one of the women bred by the Spaniards when the ships came to grief on Scottish ground. She reminded Geordie of a gazelle; elegant, graceful, with dainty movements. When he grew up, he would find a woman like her and marry her.

'Megan's puppies won't get born,' Geordie said.

'Angus will soon cure that,' Catherine McGregor said, with absolute confidence in her husband's skill. 'Come and see what he's bought for our dining-room. I don't know what he'll bring home next. He found it in that old shop at the back of Inveraray when he went there last week to cure a cow. I only hope he doesn't find a life-size statue of a horse one day or it'll come upstairs and go right through the floor. I'm sure they're all rotten. This place is an absolute barn and draughty as a stable. Brrr.'

She shivered. She always felt the cold and the big fires did little but take the chill off the place. Geordie followed her, tripping over the worn place in the Turkey runner, and, as he put his hand out to steady himself, striking the great gong so that it boomed suddenly and one of the dogs barked and all the others joined in.

19

The twins spilled out of the kitchen, sticky with toffee. Davina was almost drowned in one of Maggie's big white aprons. Maggie had 'done' for the vet for most of her life; Angus always said she would do for all of them as her ideas on hygiene were hazardous and he objected to the family socks being washed in the washing-up bowl, though Maggie said blithely you had to eat a peck of dirt before you died so what did it matter?

'Come and see what Dad's bought,' Davina said, tossing back the mass of dark hair that was held by a red ribbon. 'Honestly, you'll never guess.'

Geordie followed them, glad to be distracted. Part of him was elsewhere, listening for Megan to howl, anxiously wondering if she would survive the birth of the pups, desperately hoping for his own puppy, for something to share the quiet house with him, to play with in the garden on Grandy's bad days, and to talk to. Grandy didn't hear very well, and sometimes when he spoke to her her mind was far away, wondering what to make the boy for supper, wondering if the money would spin out and keep them both as her son had left very little, and had not insured his life. There would be money one day, in compensation, but it was a long time coming.

Donald flung open the dining-room door and switched on the light. Geordie blinked. He was used to the devil masks on the walls, and the bow and arrows, and the embroidered picture of the Queen, her face flushed hectic red, her hair an unlikely black and the jewels round her neck glittering fiercely. It had been left to Angus in a will together with a grandfather clock that didn't go, and that when wound, struck twenty-seven, and a very old donkey that brooded in the barn and had a passion for apples, stealing them unripe from the orchard until it needed treatment for greed.

Geordie stared, and the twins, unable to stand his expression any longer, shrieked with laughter. He could not think of a thing to say.

'Most families have skeletons in the cupboard,' Catherine said. 'This family has a skeleton in the dining-room.'

'His name's Horace,' Donald said. 'Dad bought him because we know all about the anatomy of dogs and cats and he thought it was time we knew about human anatomy. Besides, Davina is going to be an artist and you can't draw unless you know all about bones. Look at Michelangelo and his dissecting.'

Geordie knew very little about Michelangelo. Donald and Davina knew about the most unlikely subjects, mainly because their father was interested in so many things. There was a piece of Roman pavement in the garden; and a sundial from a mediaeval monastery in the middle of what Catherine called the weedgarden, as no one ever had time to tend it. There was an old pony trap out in the barn; and an elephant's hoof that served as an umbrella stand out on the porch.

Angus was renowned for being canny as he never paid more than fifty pence for any of his acquisitions. 'One day,' he would say, 'they'll be worth a fortune, they're investments, woman.' Catherine looked at them, sighing, and thinking of how she dusted them and kept them all clean.

'I wish they'd hurry,' Geordie said. His eyes wandered away from Horace, who he thought an awkward companion for meal times.

'You can't hurry birth,' Catherine said. 'Come away to the kitchen and have something to eat. I'll bet Andrew never remembered to feed you. He has a head with holes like a fishing net, that man, and doesn't eat enough to keep a swallow alive.'

The kitchen was along the passage and down three steps and round the corner. The warmth hit them as they opened the door. The giant Aga was turned up high, and the dogs, lying in their baskets, greeted them with barks. Sultan and Tartar, the two big Alsatians, came forward to sniff suspiciously at the stranger and then relaxed, and six-month-old Limbo, the latest Alsatian pup, bounded up to them flat-eared, all wiggle and wag, a beam on his face as he greeted Geordie, who belonged to the pup's world. The fox cub had come into the kitchen too and was prospecting for food. He hissed at Limbo who retreated, not willing to take up the challenge. Tycho had sharp teeth and a quick temper.

'I think this house should be called House of Beasts, not the vet's house,' Catherine said, as she cut giant slices off a currant cake and handed one to Geordie and one each to the twins. Davina was stirring a saucepan, muttering to herself as if casting spells, and Donald had picked up one of the stickiest of the toffee apples and was trying to chew it.

'It's set like rock,' he said and handed it to Limbo who sniffed it and walked away in disgust.

Geordie ate his cake without tasting it. He usually loved the big kitchen with the settles against the walls, padded with patchwork cushions, and littered with baskets for the animals. There was always one animal or another recovering from a birth or an operation, in one of the cages against the wall near to the Aga. Tonight a tortoiseshell cat was coming round from the anaesthetic, her leg in plaster.

'She had a road accident,' Catherine said.

Geordie scarcely heard her. The surgery door had opened and he heard the men's voices in the hall; Angus deep and loud and gruff and Andrew answering in a lighter tone. Geordie raced to meet them.

'Is Megan all right?' he asked.

'Right as rain,' Angus said. 'I had to operate. A Caesarian, poor old girl. The first pup was crossways and was dead. The other pups are alive, only . . .'

He hesitated.

'Only what?' Geordie asked.

'One of them is very small, and I don't think it will survive. I'm going to put it down,' Angus said, well aware of the boy's immediate reaction.

'You can't.' Geordie was fierce. No animal was ever going to die while he was around.

'It's no use keeping it, lad,' Andrew said gently. 'The bitch has no milk and we're going to have to hand-rear. Catherine says she will do it for me, but she can't do all of them. It's for the best.'

'My cat can rear it. She lost two of her kittens and she's lots of milk,' Geordie said.

'The cat will never take a pup,' Andrew said. 'It's no use, lad. It's too small to rear, and that's the end of it.'

'Can I see them?' Geordie asked.

Angus nodded, and the boy went into the room. Megan was lying under a lamp, stretched out, still unconscious. He looked at her, fear paramount, but she twitched a paw, and he relaxed. The pups were in a cardboard box under the heat of another lamp, beside the fire. They were moving restlessly, their mouths seeking for milk. The smallest whimpered. Geordie put his finger down in front of it and at once it was seized and sucked vigorously.

'He isn't weak at all,' Geordie said furiously. 'He's strong; it's just that he's so small. Please let me try; you're only going to put him to sleep so what does it matter if it doesn't work? Let me take him to Trippie; she loves babies. She nursed my baby rabbit when it was little.'

'But not with milk,' Angus said.

'My dad said I could have a pup this year. I want this pup.'

Andrew sighed. Children. You could never make them out. The boy could have any pup in the litter; but he had to choose the feeblest and single himself out for more heartbreak. It was useless and would never work and it was ridiculous to pretend it would.

'You can have the pup. But don't blame us if it dies,' Andrew said. No use feeding the child on dreams. Life wasn't like that.

23

'You're nuts,' Davina said. 'A sick puppy never survives.'

'It isn't sick,' Geordie said stubbornly.

'I'm leaving Megan here. If you bring that home you'll need a hot water bottle and to keep it very warm. It had better be fed first and then you can see. But suppose it lives and the cat won't feed it?'

'She will feed it,' Geordie said, totally confident. 'She can't ever resist fish. I'll smear him in fish and she'll lick him clean and then she'll feed him. She's a pig.'

'I thought she was a cat,' Davina said, but Geordie was too intent on his pup to reply. He watched while Catherine filled a hot water bottle; he fed the pup himself from the dropper when the milk was mixed, and took a carton of dried puppy food with him into the Land-Rover. The hot water bottle was tucked inside his coat. The pup was wrapped in cotton wool, tucked in beside the bottle. He could feel it moving against his hand, could feel the small wet nose, and the minute damp mouth and he sat in a daze of excitement, cradling his hand over it, all the way home.

Andrew stopped at the door.

'I wonder what your grandmother will say,' he said.

Geordie stared at the farmer. The thought had never crossed his mind. Grandy hadn't been very pleased when Trippie had kittens. She'd thought Trippie was a tom. Small animals were wild and could be noisy. And the pup would be noisy and would need a great deal of looking after.

'Will you come and tell her?' Geordie asked.

Andrew hesitated and then he shook his head. The boy had to learn to fight his own battles. The man felt very mean as he watched the small figure trudge up the garden path towards the lighted porch, his hand held firmly over the pup.

Andrew sighed.

He and Angus were both insane. They should never

24

have agreed. But it was over now. The old lady would never allow the pup into the house. It was far too small, and the work involved would be stupendous.

Geordie turned to face the Land-Rover. His face was set, too grim for a boy of eleven.

Andrew never guessed at the boy's thoughts. In that moment Geordie had determined not only to rear the pup, but to train it himself to work the sheep and to prove that it was never wise to put any pup down because the one that went had all the makings of the pick of the litter. He looked up desperately as his grandmother opened the door. He had a real fight ahead. Grandy was not very fond of dogs. Andrew drove away.

Chapter Two

Sheena Graham stared at her grandson. They were the same height: Geordie was small for his age and Sheena was a tiny woman. Her brown eyes were hostile. It had been a bad day. The arthritis in her hands and hips had drained her of energy, leaving her irritable, and she was not yet used to the change in her way of life.

She had thought she would be alone for ever, and had geared herself accordingly. Ten years of widowhood had passed, leaving her reluctant to sacrifice her independence. If there was a committee in the village, Sheena was on it, usually as chairman. When there was a petition to be presented, Sheena organised it. Her own needs were simple. The cottage she had retired to after her husband's death was small, with one spare bedroom delicately furnished to house her many friends.

Her only son had married happily. She loved his brief visits, and was fond of her daughter-in-law and of her grandson, but she had found their presence tiring and Ian had always taken his family to the local hotel.

Their death had been a terrible shock. And perhaps even worse had been the slow realisation that there was no other relative in the world to care for Geordie. Ian had been an only child and so had his wife, though Margaret had a cousin living in Manchester who had been very close to her, and who had lived with them as a child.

Jennie would have taken the boy, but Sheena was proud. No one would ever say she had refused to give a home to her orphaned grandson, but there were few people who knew the effort it cost her. She was sixty-eight; and felt, at night, when her bones ached and her body was exhausted by the extra work that Geordie caused, that she had earned a rest.

She looked now at the tiny pup in his hands, and she had no words at all. If she spoke she would snap at the boy and see again the forlorn look on his face, and feel that he was turning against her, as bewildered as she by the change in their circumstances. Ian had been a good father, close to his son. They had spent a great deal of time together, watching cricket matches, fishing and going on the long country walks that his wife had loved too.

All that had ended, snuffed out in a moment when a lorry skidded on an oil patch and its trailer jack-knifed and hit their car, and the car behind piled into it. Grandy had insisted that the boy was moved to the hospital near her as soon as possible; she had brought Trippie, the cat, home to live with them although she did not like animals; but Geordie felt a stranger still in her home, afraid of breaking the fragile ornaments, afraid of dirtying the pale carpets, afraid of making too much noise.

He looked up at her, his eyes pleading, reminding her of a dog begging for attention.

She looked down at the pup, and her heart sank. Whoever had given it to the boy must be insane. Her thoughts raced, thinking of bottle-feeds, of the needs of this small blind creature, and of the mess a puppy would make in her neat little home. Puddles and worse. How could the child have a dog? It was bad enough to have the boy there . . .

She checked her thoughts.

Angry words were boiling in her head; anger at circumstance that had given her a child to bring up when she was so old and so tired; anger at the lorry that had deprived her of her son; anger at the man who had now so thoughtlessly loaded her with extra responsibility. She had had a bad evening, fighting the welfare committee for benefits for a poor family in the village who were so feckless it was difficult to know how to cope with them. But the four children and the new baby could not be left to starve. Mary McClean, the chairman of the committee, had been against everything that Sheena proposed. She and Mary never agreed over anything, but Mary was younger and forceful and had carried the motion, and Sheena was worried about the children. Never mind the parents; it was the children that mattered.

And now Geordie had brought her new worries.

She led the way indoors. His glass of hot milk, and two biscuits, were waiting for him on the table beside the fire. He hated hot milk; but he dared not tell his grandmother. She worried about his small size and tried to feed him up, not realising he had inherited his build from her and not from her son, who had taken after her husband's family.

Geordie did not know what to say. Words milled in his mind, but panic stopped them from being spoken. If he didn't ask, she couldn't say 'no'. If he took it for granted that he could keep and feed the pup, perhaps everything would be all right. He sought for omens. If a piece of wood at the back of the fire sparked to sudden life, everything would be all right; if the cat came to inspect the pup; if he could count to one hundred before Grandy spoke.

Sheena was counting to a hundred too. The night before she had chided Geordie for untidiness and he had exploded at her, shouting at her that he hated her and her silly little house, and the awful ornaments that broke if he only looked at them.

'All you ever say is "no",' he had shouted. 'No, you can't go and play with the twins; no, you mustn't worry Andrew, he's busy; no, you are not to go and spend so much time with Faceache; and there you go again, telling me to call him Mr Fazackerley; I hate being here; I wish I'd died with my mother and father.'

He had stormed upstairs to fling himself on his bed, sobbing noisily. Sheena, not knowing what to do or say, had left him alone. The outburst would do him good. He hadn't cried; hadn't seemed to care that his parents were both dead; had shown so little emotion that she had been worried.

But the scene had left her drained and exhausted and she could not face another. She sat, trying to collect her thoughts, while Geordie nursed the pup against him and sipped at his milk, every swallow an ordeal.

Sheena stood up, easing herself painfully from her chair. She went out into the kitchen to try to find a quiet place, away from the sight of the child, to rally her thoughts. Somehow, thinking seemed difficult these days, and there was too much to do, all the time. Geordie needed so much food. He got his clothes so dirty. She had long forgotten about boys' clothes, and mud and mess. And the house needed cleaning up three times a day; untidiness bothered her after all these years alone. She longed to be alone again and then guilt needled; there was nowhere else for the child to go.

Why me, she thought wearily. Why couldn't it have happened to Mary McClean; she could manage a house full of children and never even notice them, with her efficiency and bustling busyness and it might keep her off committees and interfering where she shouldn't.

It was no good. Thinking round in circles solved nothing. She poured herself a glass of cold milk and went back into the tiny sitting-room that seemed so much smaller with Geordie there, and with Trippie and her kittens.

She hadn't wanted the cat, but had known that at least one link with his past life would help the boy; and Trippie had been the only link possible. She was horrified when she realised that the cat was not only female but in kitten by the time Geordie was beginning to be about again. The kittens were now four weeks old. Mercifully Trippie was beautifully clean and had trained her own kits, but they were mischievous and weaning them was much more trouble than she had realised.

And now the pup.

29

Oh Geordie, Geordie lad, she thought helplessly. If only you were older; or had been a girl. I'm too old to bring up another lad.

Geordie was kneeling by Trippie's box. Trippie, fluffed to three times her normal size, outraged by the smell of pup, was hissing at the boy for daring to bring this intruder among her clean kits. Geordie held the pup against the cat. Her swift paw, claws outstretched, scratched the tiny head, bringing blood. The four kittens, copying their mother, arched and spat too.

It wasn't going to work.

'Geordie, you cannot make her take the pup. She'll kill it,' Sheena said. 'It hasn't a chance of life, lad. Ye'll have to take it back to the bitch. I cannot think what Andrew was about, letting you bring the wee thing here.'

'Megan hasn't any milk. They were going to put this one down, but I wanted it,' Geordie said.

'Geordie . . .'

'My father said I could have a dog for my birthday this year. I didn't have one. I was in hospital. It isn't my fault I'm not at home. I can't have anything. You never let me have anything. I want my dog. I want something to play with. You don't let me go out and play in case I get hurt . . .'

His voice was rising and Sheena knew she couldn't stand it again. The months of suppression were over; reality was beginning to hurt. Perhaps at first disaster numbed the victim and only after a while did the truth strike through a shell built up by the body as a defence against something too unspeakable to appreciate in its entirety. Somehow in these last few weeks she too had begun to feel her son's loss more.

At first she had been carried along by the sheer necessity of doing things; of selling his home, of going through his papers; of visiting Geordie in hospital. The funeral had been unreal; and the sympathetic visits of her friends. Now, the months that had passed were almost forgotten but the present was becoming increasingly harassing. There was so much of Geordie and even with a lame leg he seemed to rush everywhere, thumping on the floor, slamming doors, muddling wherever he went. She had married late and found her own son something of a problem, and been secretly thankful when he made his own life and she could rebuild hers, carefully occupying every hour and armouring herself against loneliness.

'It's a bad scratch,' Geordie said forlornly. The cat's claw had caught in the tiny skull, tearing the skin.

'You can feed it and keep it alive tonight, but in the morning it goes back to Angus or to Andrew,' Sheena said. 'Geordie, if Trippie won't take it, it will have to be fed every two hours, day and night for over three weeks; how are we going to do that?'

'I can do the feeds; I'll set my clock,' Geordie said.

'And what about school? Do you sleep all day at your lessons? And how do I clean the house and look after a wee helpless motherless pup? And wash our clothes? And do the cooking and the shopping and all there is to do about the place? You must be sensible, lad.'

The pup moved its head, seeking for warmth and food. Its small blind head nuzzled against Geordie's warm woollen jersey. The tiny mouth fastened on to his finger and sucked.

'It's time for food,' Geordie said.

He tucked the pup carefully into his pocket, its head peeping out. He refused to understand his grandmother's words. He went out and prepared the feed, measuring meticulously. Andrew had given him a dropper to use for the first few days. He would have to drip the milk down the pup's throat; and be careful not to drip it into its lungs instead of its gullet.

He sat back in the chair, wrapping the tiny creature in a thick wad of paper tissues, holding it delicately, every sense concentrated on what he was doing. The pup was hungry, and opened its mouth greedily for the milk. The boy's brown eyes were grave, giving no sign of the intense pleasure that the child felt. He had no intention whatever of returning the pup to Andrew, who would only have it put to sleep. Megan couldn't feed it; Trippie wouldn't feed it; and Catherine hadn't time. He had not realised before how long the feeding would take.

Each drop had to be placed accurately on the small tongue, and he had to wait till the pup had swallowed. It had taken ten minutes to prepare the feed and to cool it; and everything had to be sterilised. Catherine had shown him how.

Drop by tiny drop, with the pup swallowing and opening his small mouth for more. There was only an inch of milk in the pipette, but even so it took nearly fifteen minutes to get it down and then the pup had to be massaged, or he wouldn't function at all and would die by retaining his own wastes.

Angus had given Geordie a thick paintbrush, which he dipped in olive oil, warmed in a saucer he had placed in the hearth. Rub, rub, rub, like a softly-licking mother's tongue, until at last he achieved the result he wanted and cleaned the tiny animal and tucked it into his shirt again.

There was nothing so obstinate as a boy, Sheena thought with exasperation, never realising that her grandson had inherited her own tenacity of purpose. She went out into the kitchen and looked in the cupboard where paper and string and boxes were neatly stacked, ready for packing Christmas presents. She threw nothing away that might come in useful and was thankful that she had kept many of her son's good clothes, packed away in a trunk for the day when his own son was big enough for them. The jerseys were almost as good as new, and saved her a great deal of money.

She found a shoe box, and lined it with thick cotton wool, and fetched a small hot water bag, that she used for her back when it was bad, and filled it, lying it carefully under the cotton wool, covering everything with a woollen

32

square of blanket, hoarded to make a duster or a floor-cloth.

Geordie's vivid smile was an unlooked-for reward, and for a moment her resolve faltered.

'He goes back in the morning,' she said. 'But I'll feed him for you at midnight and you can get up at two. I'll do the four o'clock feed. Heaven knows what you'll be like at school tomorrow. But I'll not change my mind, so don't set your heart on keeping the pup.'

Geordie put the pup in the box. It looked very small.

Sheena put the guard against the fire. She would have to watch the cat. And the kittens. They had needle-like claws.

Geordie kissed her goodnight, a dutiful peck on the soft wrinkled cheek. Sheena had never been a demonstrative woman. Geordie missed his mother's bear hugs and her warm greeting when he came home from school, her frequent laughter and her blithe disregard of untidiness. Margaret had been untidy herself. She would have liked a basketful of babies but Geordie was all she got, and there was no hope of others. Both she and her husband tried to make up to the boy for his lack of brothers and sisters by letting him fill the house with his friends.

He missed them. Tubby and Gareth and Fatty Smythe and Tommo. They had been inseparable. He would have loved to spend more time with Donald and Davina but there was no bus or train link between the two villages and he could only visit when someone was going over by car and willing to have a boy as passenger. And his grandmother would not let him ask.

He sat on the edge of his bed, worrying about the pup. It needed something to snuggle against. He opened the trunk in his room. He hadn't looked inside since it arrived, not wanting to rouse memories.

Grandy had packed all his old toys.

The teddy bear with one eye and a tatty red knitted suit that Trippie had eaten into holes, loving wool. The aged furry camel. The tractor his father had bought him that last Christmas, more as a joke as it was much too young a toy.

It had to be somewhere.

Geordie rummaged frantically, wishing he had no memories. He didn't want to revive them; didn't want to think of his mother laughing as he opened parcels at Christmas, her bright eyes watching him, knowing he would feel pleasure at their carefully chosen gifts.

He swallowed the lump in his throat.

The toy he was looking for had been one he loved most and that he could least bear to handle. His mother had knitted it for him. She was a bad knitter and hid her efforts from Grandy, who was critical. But the woolly donkey would be perfect for the pup. He could nestle between its soft floppy legs and nuzzle against it.

It was there, in the corner of the trunk, right at the bottom, between an outgrown pair of football boots and his football. He remembered playing with his father the day before the crash. He pushed the memory away. The pup was important. He grabbed Old Flop, and ran downstairs.

His grandmother was sitting in the chair, her eyes closed. She jumped as he came in.

'This will make him feel safer,' Geordie said, and held the untidy woollen toy to the fire to warm it. He tucked it into the box. It took up most of the space, and the pup, instinct already strong in his small black and white body, scrambled towards the bulk and wriggled himself between the long woolly legs, and tried to nurse from the soft underbody.

A moment later, warm, fed, and secure, he was asleep.

Geordie looked down, and then knelt and, very gently, stroked the soft, almost invisible fur. Sheena watched him, and looked away. It was useless to pretend they could keep the little animal.

Trippie, coming to the hearthrug to gain warmth from

the fire, saw the pup and spat again.

There were too many problems and she was too old.

'Bed, Geordie, fast,' Sheena said.

The door closed behind her grandson.

There was no comfort in solitude.

Trippie stalked the box and Sheena lifted it on to the table beside her, and at last took the cat's basket and the kittens into the next room. She had to put on the electric fire. It was much too cold for them. That would mean more expense.

She returned to put the pup's box down again on the hearthrug. He was quite still and for a moment she hoped he had died. But when she stooped she could hear the faint flutter of his breath. So nothing was solved.

The minutes ticked by.

A coal fell, and then, startlingly, came a tap at the window. Terrified, Sheena stared at the drawn curtains. No one could possibly be calling at this hour of night. It was a quarter to midnight. She could not move.

The tap came again.

It was absurd. She nerved herself to walk over and draw back the curtain and then felt unreasonably angry as she recognised Tom Fazackerley, Andrew's stockman. Tom was as old as she but a sight spryer; no one would think he was nearly seventy. They had been at school together. Tom had pulled her pigtails and she had hit him in rage. He had laughed at her, the girl from the manse, little Mistress Proper, while his father was the village villain, unable to resist taking pheasants and salmon that rightly belonged to the Laird.

Sheena opened the front door.

Tom came in. He was grizzled in hair and brows, with unnervingly bright blue eyes that stared straight into her mind and read it accurately, as they always had. He had been an awkward playmate at school and he had been an awkward kind of man ever since, always outspoken, and totally unaware that anyone was better than he. And

35

maybe he was right at that, Sheena thought; he is as good a man as my father was, for all his own father's back-slidings.

Tom walked into the sitting-room, dwarfing the room even more than Geordie did.

'So the lad won?' Tom said.

'Of course not. But I can't let the creature die, nor can I leave it unfed till morning,' Sheena said tartly.

'I told him he was mad,' Tom said. He never referred to Andrew by name. 'Told him you'd never agree. Told him it would mean heartbreak for the lad. And it will. Geordie's been set on a pup ever since he found Megan was in whelp.'

'And you encouraged him, no doubt,' Sheena said.

'That I did not, Sheena Graham. You always were one for hasty judgements and unfair ones,' Tom said. 'I told him; but Geordie is as stubborn as you. Diamond cut diamond the pair of you, I reckon.'

Sheena said nothing. What answer was there?

'The lad's had a raw deal,' Tom said. 'And he's had the pup long enough to mind too much if it's taken from him. I'll come and do the night feeds if ye'll do the day feeds. I can cat nap; I don't sleep well these days as it is. Bones complaining and I have to walk around or I get too stiff. Let the lad keep the pup. You'll not regret it.'

'And when it starts running around?' Sheena asked. 'Puddles on the carpets and torn up clothes and chewing at things; what then? I don't like my home messed up.'

'Houses were made for people, not people for houses,' Tom said. 'What do you want, a shrine where no one walks, and no dust settles, or a place where the boy finds a refuge from the world outside? Its treated him rough; he needs to lick his wounds; and grow a new skin; and he won't do it with you nagging him, Sheena Graham. Do you want him to remember you for ever telling him to clean his shoes and tidy his room and mind his noise, or do you want him to remember you gave him a home

36

when his was snatched from him?'

Sheena stared at him, her mouth set. Tom always had a way of bringing out unpalatable facts.

'Get to your bed, and think about it,' Tom said. 'I'd like the boy to keep the wee creature. It will give him something to think about beside himself and teach him responsibility. And give him something to care for; he needs a dog of his own more than any boy I know.'

'Couldn't you take it till it's house-trained?' Sheena asked.

'And do him out of the teaching?' Tom shook his head. 'He has to learn himself; no one can do it for him. He wants a dog. He has to know what having a dog's about. No use spoon feeding him. Let him do his own growing up. You can't protect him for ever; and you mustn't baby him. He's eleven years old. And he needs to run wild; let him run wild with a dog beside him. It'll teach him more than you've ever learned, Sheena Graham.'

'Make yourself a drink,' Sheena said, hating him. She left the room and went wearily to her bed, where she lay awake watching the pattern of bare branched trees flung by moonlight on her wall, and fell asleep at last to dream uneasily of Geordie taunting her with her indifference, and shouting 'I hate you. I hate you. I hate you.'

She woke to find the shouting was real and Geordie was standing beside her bed.

'Geordie!' She was only half awake and she couldn't understand what he was saying.

'You didn't wake me. The pup will be dead.'

'Geordie!'

It was Tom's voice from downstairs.

Geordie ran out on to the landing and stared at the man.

'You'll apologise to your grandmother and stop behaving like a spoiled bairn.' Tom never minced words. 'I fed the pup and it's fine except for that scratch on its head which is swollen; Angus will do something about that.

37

Come down and give it a feed before you eat. Go back and apologise first!'

Tom went back into the room to mend the fire. Geordie crept meekly in to his grandmother's bedroom again.

'I'm sorry,' he said.

'You didn't know. I'll be up soon and make your breakfast, lad.'

She was stiff and every bone in her body ached, but she would have to get up, and face the day again.

Geordie went downstairs. Tom had the kettle on and the feed made up ready for him. Bacon sizzled in the pan and toast browned under the grill. The table was laid for two.

Geordie went back into the room. The skin on the pup's head was puffy; the scratch had a yellow crust on it. But the pup fed well, taking each drop and swallowing, knowing now what it must do.

'I should try it on the bottle, lad. Less chance of the milk going down the wrong way,' Tom said and watched approvingly as Geordie finished giving the feed and massaged the pup and cleaned it up, and then sat it against his hand to break the wind that filled it. It burped noisily and Geordie laughed.

'It's strong,' he said.

'Aye, strong enough, even though it's small,' Tom said. 'But don't bank on keeping it, lad. I don't like the look of that scratch and it's far from easy to hand-rear a wee creature. Its early days, and for the first month it's better not to hope too much. There's many a slip . . .'

Tom was a great quoter of clichés.

There was a robin on the windowsill. Geordie watched it, looking for an omen. If it hopped to the right, the pup would live; if it hopped to the left, the pup would die. He held his breath. Trippie stalked across the garden. The robin saw her and flew off, neither left nor right, but straight out and up.

Geordie sighed and let out his breath.

38

What kind of omen was that?

The pup settled comfortably against Old Flop. Tom grinned as the little creature tucked itself hard against the woollen body and tried to nuzzle, its blind head seeking and sniffing as it looked for milk. Within moments it was still, sleeping with its head on the round plump belly of the toy.

'That was a brainwave,' Tom said. 'Now come and make a tray for your grandmother and take her her breakfast in bed. Time she had a bit of fussing. Where's the traycloth?'

Geordie laid the tray carefully. His grandmother liked everything just so. He found the pretty plate and cup and saucer that she loved and rarely used and Tom made paper thin toast and cut it into fingers, and made tea, and boiled an egg for just three minutes.

He carried the tray upstairs and gave it to Geordie when he reached the landing.

Sheena was making up her mind to dress when Geordie came into the room. She stared at the tray.

'Faceache thought you'd like your breakfast in bed for once,' Geordie said cheerfully. 'The pup's fine.'

He wouldn't mention the scratch on its head. It would heal; small animals healed easily. He couldn't lose it now.

'That's lovely, Geordie,' Sheena said gratefully, as she sat up. 'It's just what I needed.'

A rest; a break; and someone to think for her for a little while. Geordie balanced the tray carefully on his grandmother's knees and gave her the soft stole that she wore when reading in bed. He switched on the electric fire. The room was cold.

'Tom says he'll help with the pup,' Sheena said and was rewarded by an impulsive hug that almost upset her tea in her lap.

'I won't let it be a nuisance, I promise,' Geordie said and went downstairs with dreams of a dog at his side, obedient and perfectly trained, following him at heel,

39

sitting at the flick of a finger, racing with him along the beach, sleeping on the floor beside his bed at night, guarding him from danger.

The thoughts buoyed him through the day.

The pup fed. Trippie, banished to the other room, kept her distance. Geordie was taking no chances, though Sheena worried about the fuel bills. The rooms needed to be kept very warm for all the small animals. And the pup's food was expensive; and it would need more and more. Her thoughts were racing, as she tried to replan her budget. If only legal affairs didn't take so long. She would have to speak to the bank manager again.

The worry grew during the day.

Geordie, unaware of his grandmother's fears, had one of his own. By teatime, the skin round the scratch was obviously puffy and swollen and he could no longer pretend that there was nothing wrong.

He left his grandmother in charge after tea and went to find Andrew, who came home with him and bent to look at the tiny creature.

'Trippie scratched him when I tried to make her feed him,' Geordie said forlornly.

'That was very bad luck. I think we'll have to take him to Angus,' Andrew said.

'He'll get cold.'

'Put a hot water bag on your lap, and tuck the pup in a pair of old socks and I'll put the heater full on,' Andrew said. 'But Geordie, no promises. It's very difficult to rear such a small animal and an infection on the head at this stage could be very dangerous. Promise me if Angus says he must be put to sleep that you'll say yes.'

The thought was unbearable. Geordie wrapped the pup in his warm socks, and Tom filled the hot water bag and wrapped that in the blanket scrap. Very carefully, Geordie walked out to the Land-Rover. He saw nothing on the drive but the small black and white head; he knew every detail of the small ears, of the tiny paws and the fragile

40

claws; the fluttering breathing frightened him. Was it growing less strong? Was the small heart thudding erratically? Was the new life slipping away under his hands, so that all his work had been in vain?

Angus had just finished surgery when they arrived. He looked down at Geordie.

'Trouble already?' he asked.

Geordie could only nod.

Angus took them into the surgery. Geordie leaned against the medicine cupboard, watching Angus set the pup on its back on the table, still wrapped warmly in the socks and lying on the hot water bag.

He bent to look at the scratch.

'I'm sorry, lad,' he said. 'It's formed a wee abscess. There's not a chance in Hades of saving this pup's life. It will never survive. Let me put it down now, before you're too fond of it.'

'You can inject it,' Geordie said. 'Dogs don't die of abscesses.'

'Geordie, have some sense.'

'Please,' Geordie said. 'Please, just try.'

Angus shook his head.

'It's impossible, lad.' The vet sighed and wondered how on earth he would ever get through to the boy. 'I couldn't even work out the dose for a pup as small as that. I could just as easily kill it with an injection as cure it. I've never tried to save one this age. It isn't sense.'

'Then you're just a murderer,' Geordie said fiercely. 'You won't even try. Please, please, please.'

Angus went to the cupboard and took out a hypodermic syringe. He measured a minute dose of antibiotic into it, and took the pup and injected it. He cleaned the cut on the head and gave the wee creature back to the boy.

'That's all I can do,' he said. 'My guess is that it will be dead by morning. It hasn't a chance. It would be kinder to put it down now, before it begins to suffer.'

'I suffered in hospital,' Geordie said, suddenly remembering agonised days and nights and the wicked pain when his injuries were dressed. 'Nobody put me to sleep.'

Angus looked at Andrew, and shook his head. Andrew shrugged. The boy had to learn. If not one way then he had to learn the other.

Neither of them said a word on the journey home. Geordie felt the fragile breath move the sleeping pup and could not even speak. And Andrew dared not.

Chapter Three

Sheena Graham had nothing to say when they returned. Life had caught her up again; she had thought to retire and end her days in peace; and now she was realising that this was an impossible dream. Perhaps peace was illusory after all, she thought. Maybe one couldn't ever plan; shouldn't ever plan. The best laid schemes of mice and men . . .

She busied herself, preparing the pup's feed. Geordie had nothing to say either. He was praying, inside his head, so hard that he had room for no other thought. Please God, let the puppy live. Please God, please God. Just this once let me have something happen right. I'll work at school; I'll be good; I will, I promise.

Andrew Grant paused at the door and looked at Sheena. Tom had told him off properly the night before when they were mucking out the sow, a vast, prolific creature that Tom had named Queenie, saying she was the queen of his heart. Sometimes Andrew thought the man cared more for the pig than for any human creature, brooding over her when she was about to farrow and absurdly proud of the squealing piglets that she produced without effort at regular intervals.

Tom was staring at Queenie, as Andrew approached.

'He's as daft as any creature I ever met,' he told the sow, knowing well that his employer was behind him. 'Giving that wee useless thing to a lad barely eleven years old with no one but an old lady to bring him up. What kind of sense is that? The pup will die; the lad will be desolate and the woman will suffer some more as Geordie's a passionate lad, and doesn't know how to hold his tongue. And he's had a bad time.'

Andrew had stopped in his tracks. He had not been thinking of Sheena at all. He had thought that the need to look after the pup would help the boy; give him something to think about beyond himself. Andrew had recognised the signs of grief that Sheena had missed, knowing how he himself had shown no sign to anyone of the hurt he felt when his young wife had died. The boy hid his feelings and showed an unnatural restraint for his age, rarely shouting or playing, far too sober for his age.

A dog would help that. The boy would learn to play again, to run and to romp and to take the edge off his energy, and he would learn discipline too in the need to care for an animal.

Andrew had hoped the cat would accept the pup and there would be few problems. He had not thought at all. He was savagely angry at himself. Sheena Graham was not farm-bred and she avoided animals. And he had forgotten how old she was. She was very young for her years, and would easily pass for fifty, but she was almost seventy and he should have remembered.

He did not know how to apologise. He drove up to the cottage.

It was easiest after all to say the truth.

'I am sorry, Mrs Graham. I did not think . . .'

Sheena looked at him, and saw the unhappiness in his eyes.

'Neither did I, Andrew. It will do the boy good; he has to learn about living. And he has to live with me, so I must do my share.'

She paused, wanting to add that she found it difficult, but Andrew was troubled enough and she would not add to his worries.

'Tom's promised to help. We'll manage,' she said.

For all that, as she went back into the sitting-room, she found herself wishing again that the pup would die and solve her problem. She could not face a dog as well as a boy about the house.

Geordie had re-filled the hot water bag and put it at the bottom of the shoe box. The pup was tucked in between Old Flop's saggy legs, its small body dark against the creamy wool. It was sound asleep, breathing faintly, a bare flutter of the small sides. Geordie was kneeling above it, all his feelings in his eyes. Sheena could not bear to look at him.

She went out into the kitchen and busied herself with making his favourite tea, a meal she felt so badly balanced and totally indigestible, that she rarely made it for him, though his mother had often let him choose his supper and had never worried about diet, knowing that an occasional binge did little harm to a healthy appetite.

'You must eat, Geordie,' Sheena said, going back into the room. 'The injection will make the pup sleep and it's not time for its feed yet. Come on.'

Geordie looked at the plate.

Two fried eggs and baked beans and chips, crisp and golden, just the way his mother had made them, cut with a crinkly edge. There was a lump in his throat and he swallowed, shaken by an intense wish to be back again, safe, a year ago, when they had all been together. His father would have shouted 'Boy, egg and chips,' and swung him high in the air, laughing, and his mother would have said impatiently 'Come on and eat while it's hot. I've been in the kitchen all day . . .' and both he and his father would immediately chant 'working my fingers to the bone,' so that they ended in laughter again.

He began to eat.

He was very hungry, and gradually the food erased memory. He managed to smile at his grandmother, knowing she had cooked this specially for him, by way of apology. She had often remonstrated with his mother for feeding the boy such an indigestible meal at night.

'The pup's got an abscess,' Geordie said.

Sheena looked down at it. Two days old; how could it possibly live? Supposing the infection damaged the brain?

Supposing the boy was infected by the poison causing the abscess? Or she herself? The worry nagged her while she was washing up; and flared again when Geordie lifted the pup for its evening feed.

It was very sleepy. The teat slipped out of the tiny mouth and it would not suck. Geordie tried again and again and at last made up fresh food; the milk was a nuisance to mix and formed into lumps unless he was very careful. He shook the dropper, and returned to pick up the pup and try again.

The milk lay on the small tongue; dripped out of the sides of the tiny mouth; one drop went into the little creature's ear, and Geordie was almost in tears when Tom arrived, bringing Megan with him.

'She hasn't any milk. But maybe she can mother the wee beast,' Tom said.

Sheena, coming into the room, set her mouth when she saw the bitch.

'You needn't look like that,' Tom said. 'She's as clean as you are. She hasn't fleas and she might be what the pup is needing. She has to work during the day; seeing she's no pups to rear. But she's fretting and the pup needs a mother and he is letting her come for the night. She will warm the pup and lick him; Geordie can't get him clean enough and olive oil isn't any substitute for his mother's tongue. I've brought her basket; I'll fetch it. He lent me the Land-Rover to carry it in.'

Megan sniffed the room. She went, unerringly, to Geordie and sniffed at the pup. When Tom came back the bitch had taken it firmly in her mouth, had settled herself on the rug, and the pup was tucked against her. Within seconds, his small nose was working, his head was pushing against the sleek black fur, and he was trying to nurse.

'Will that bring her milk back?' Geordie asked.

Tom shook his head.

'But it might stimulate him to take his food,' he said.

46

'Get down on the rug beside her, Geordie, and try to feed him now.'

Geordie put his hand around the pup. Megan watched, wise-eyed, as if she knew what he was going to do. When milk spilled from the tiny mouth, she leaned her head forward and licked it clean. The pup needed his throat stroking before he would swallow.

The milk in the dropper cooled, and Tom patiently brought hot water and warmed it again, pouring it over the tube while Geordie held it.

Megan licked the pup, her warm tongue massaging its tiny body. Her expression, which had been anxious, was now blissful. Geordie, watching her, thought that if a dog could purr, Megan would be purring at the top of her voice. Once she grunted, a low, soft, contented sound. The pup stirred against her and lifted his head. She licked the tiny nose.

'Now try,' Tom said.

Geordie knelt again. This time, the small mouth opened of its own accord and the pup swallowed. He took the whole feed. Megan rolled him on his back and began her ministrations. Lick, lick, lick. When he was quite clean she nuzzled him, and nudged him against her.

Tom put the basket down beside her, in front of the fire. It was lined with a thick white towel. She lifted the pup, and stepped in, cuddling it down again. Within seconds, both bitch and pup were still, the pup's small sides lifting and sinking, lifting and sinking, in steady breathing.

'Now we just have to wait and see if that scratch will settle,' Tom said.

Sheena was crocheting, sitting on the settee, aware that the atmosphere in the room had changed. Geordie could not take his eyes off the bitch and the pup; Tom was stroking his empty pipe, a slight smile on his face; the ticking clock was a soothing background to a room that suddenly seemed more complete than she had known it.

47

The basket on the hearth; the boy's absorption; the man's satisfaction; the place was a home again. She had been without roots or people belonging for so long that she had forgotten the small happinesses that came briefly amid all the work.

Geordie looked up at her, and she smiled, a sudden warm smile.

'Bedtime, Geordie,' she said.

The boy looked at the clock. He kissed his grandmother goodnight and said goodnight to Tom, who nodded. The door closed.

'It does not take much to please a child,' Tom said.

He continued to watch the animals, thinking about his own life. Birth and death; small creatures sucking; the feeling of a mother animal for her young; the vixen for her cub; the sheep for her lamb; the cow for the calf; the mare for the foal; Queenie alone seemed to have little mother love for her frequent litters. Yet she would protect them if danger threatened, of that Tom was sure.

'Birth and death; that's what life's about,' he observed, sucking on the empty pipe, knowing Sheena hated the reek of tobacco smoke, and his old pipe was fouler than most. 'That's what matters and money isn't part of it. People forget what's important. Enough to eat; and a fire to warm you; and the beasts about you. And to know at the end that you did your best and cheated nobody.'

Sheena's busy hook flew in and out of the growing shawl. She had discovered that the shop in Inveraray would take anything she made, and it helped with the housekeeping. The work was delicate, but needed little concentration except for the patterning around the edge, a band of flowers crocheted in among the otherwise plain and filmy stitching.

There was no need to talk. Tom watched the animals, and Sheena worked until it was time for the next feed, which she made, and Tom gave. The pup fed without fuss, and the bitch licked him clean. He would have his mother at night; and he would not grow up a loner, unable to meet other dogs, for pups brought up without companions often became unsociable and sometimes savage animals. Things had a way of working out, Tom thought.

At bedtime, Sheena brought down two blankets and a pillow.

'You can stretch out on the sofa,' she said, and Tom, removing his shoes and tie after she had gone, was glad to do so, and lie in the silent room, thinking of past animals; of the bitch he had had after he was married, and the pups she had; and her way with them. Brandy had never wanted them in the basket he set for her; she had the first litter in the haystack and a rare time he had finding her; and the second litter was produced in the clean linen basket on top of the week's wash. How his wife had carried on.

By morning, the pup was obviously stronger. Geordie was downstairs by half past five, creeping into the room, where Tom was dozing. The man woke and stretched himself, and folded the blankets.

'You're an early riser,' he said.

Geordie did not hear him. He was on his knees beside the basket, making sure the pup was breathing. The small head lifted and nosed his hand, catching a finger and sucking vigorously. The scratch was clean; the swelling around it gone. Megan licked the wound with her tongue.

'That's what he needed, more than anything in the world. Every young thing needs a mother,' Tom said, and then could have cut off his hand as he saw the stillness settle on the boy's face.

'The beastie's hungry. Make its feed now,' he said, to distract Geordie, and went outside with the boy and kept up a running commentary to tide over the awkwardness and ease the hurt.

'He'll take the bottle now,' Tom said. 'Being with his mother has roused his instincts.'

This time Geordie took the pup on his lap again. Megan

left her basket and sat beside him, watching anxiously, nosing the pup constantly, licking away dribbles of milk. The pup sucked vigorously, its paws scrabbling against Geordie's hand.

'That's what it would do with Megan; push against her and release the milk,' Tom said.

There was intense satisfaction in feeding the pup; in seeing how it had strengthened overnight; in handing it back to Megan who took it delicately in her jaws and settled with it in the basket, licking it all over to wash it, to massage it, to empty it. She licked it clean and nosed it against her again, sighing deeply as it nursed at her dry teats. She had always been a good mother.

The days settled into a pattern. Geordie fed the pup before he went to school; Tom left with Megan; and Sheena put the pup back with Old Flop. She had, against her will, become interested in it and involved with it, now wanting it to live as much as Geordie did. She would never have believed it possible to be fond of an animal. Trippie she tolerated, but this minute creature had been part of her life from its birth, and as it grew, each day it became more interesting.

She was alone when it opened one eye and stared at her, through a blue haze. Geordie was home in time to see the second eye open, some hours later, and was sure the pup knew him, as it always lifted its nose to his face to smell him when he handled it, and, as he bent over Old Flop, it crawled across the box to nuzzle his hand hopefully.

By now it was taking more food and taking it well. That night it crawled to Megan, across Geordie's knee, greeting her with a lifted face. It was now obviously a small sheepdog, black and white, sleekly shining from Megan's administrations. There was a white mark down the centre of the black nose.

'A flash of white. I'm going to call him Flash,' Geordie said.

Flash grew and became a personality. A small imperious and demanding personality, hungry, shouting for food with shrill squeaks. By the time he was four weeks old he was a ball of black and white fluff, stumbling eagerly to greet Megan when she came at night, with a lick of the hand for Tom. He knew Geordie and he came to meet Sheena when she brought his bottle. Tom had rolled the carpet back near the fire and the floor was spread with thick layers of newspaper. It was easy to lift and Sheena found she did not care all that much about her previously immaculate room being turned upside down. Geordie was so much easier to live with, was eager and responsive and talked to her freely, ran home every day to feed his pup, and had woken out of his nightmare to take part in school lessons again.

He even took his football out of the trunk, and began to play with it, dribbling it round the tiny lawn at the weekends while the pup slept, tucked up comfortably against Old Flop.

Trippie's kittens had gone to new homes, and Trippie herself now tolerated the newcomer, though she would not yet come close. For one thing, Flash was becoming mischievous. With each day, he mastered movement. With each day, he made new discoveries. He found the hearth brush, which he could drag across the newspaper. It made a delicious rustling noise.

He also discovered smells. Smells that made his mouth water. He discovered that people ate, and sat towering above him, with wonderful scent drifting down to him so that he nudged Geordie's shoe, begging for a titbit which he was never allowed.

He discovered meat for himself when he was four weeks old; a tiny half teaspoonful of mince in gravy; a delectable taste that made his mouth water every time the dish appeared.

Sheena found a new pleasure in shared amusement. The pup was a constant source of laughter. His astonishment was immense when he discovered that the box on the table could make a noise at him; sometimes it spoke to him, so that he turned in amazement as a male voice suddenly sounded in the room, yet no one else had come in.

They could not decide whether he loved or hated singing, as he always joined in, a small background howl that made Sheena and Tom laugh and reduced Geordie to near hysterics. Andrew, calling in one night when a concert was in progress, with Flash, now nearly six weeks old, sitting and adding his contribution, was delighted to discover that his gift had after all been a good one; the pup was strong, although unbelievably tiny, almost a miniature, in spite of the vitamin powder that Angus had sent over by the mail van a few days before. Dougal Burns, the postman, had come in to meet the pup and make its acquaintance, so that he would not be a target for its teeth when it grew up. Now Dougal rang daily and fussed and fondled the little beast, who regarded the postman as one of his greatest friends.

By the time the pup had had his inoculations, he was showing signs of future beauty. His coat was dense and long, the fur on back and tail and legs deep glossy black. His chest and shoulders were white; and so was the tip of his right front paw. He had a straight white line from forehead to the tip of his muzzle and one white spot below his left ear. His ears were set wide on his head, and when he was puzzled he sat with one forward, one back and his forehead wrinkled, trying to make out something that was new to his life.

Television mystified him. He would sit in front of the set, head on first one side and then the other, ears moving as he listened, and then stalk slowly up to it. He would sit, almost on top of the screen, until there was a sudden movement, when he would bark, and rush under a chair. Only after some minutes had passed would he venture out again.

He was nine weeks old when Geordie discovered that

Flash was obsessed by shadows. They were walking down the garden path when Sheena switched on a light indoors. Their shadows sprang on to the ground in front of them, Geordie's long and thin and Flash's small and oddly angled.

The pup leaped on it and growled.

The shadows moved.

Flash froze, and stared up at Geordie, who was watching him, grinning. He had never thought of shadows before.

They walked across the lawn. The pup became aware there were other shadows. Shadow of a moving branch; of a long creeper moving gently in the breeze; dappled shadows under the trees.

Sometimes the pup pounced on them. Sometimes he just sat, an amused expression on his face, as the wind sang through the branches and created wildly waving darknesses on the ground, teasing him with a bewildering nothingness that he could not catch and could not smell, and that was always around him at night.

Indoors, he sometimes stalked, not Trippie, but Trippie's shadow, which was much more mystifying as it changed shape. It ran along the wainscot, it darted up the wall as Trippie leaped to the back of a chair, and the pup stood with his paws against the patterned paper, trying to make out where it had gone, as it vanished as soon as Trippie settled herself.

By the time the pup was fully weaned and Tom had ceased to come regularly at night, Sheena and Geordie often switched off the lights and sat in the dancing fire-light, watching Flash prowl along the floor, and sit, absorbed, opposite the glass fronted book case where a second fire flared and flickered and died, the dark spines of the books acting as a mirror.

Tom called in several times a week, and sat with them. Sheena had never known the man well; he had been part of her schooldays, but since then they had lived very different lives. She enjoyed talking to him. Time spent working out of doors, on his own or with animals, had given him his own philosophy. The passing days and years meant little to him in terms of age. His life had been made up of a long succession of beasts, that had been born and cared for and died, so that the Second World War began for Tom the year the old bull was put down with a growth in his brain and it ended the day that Midge had twin foals, an event so rare in the horse world that it was memorable for ever and worth writing about to a farming magazine.

The year had a different meaning for Tom too; seed-time and harvest; lambing time; the first cuckoo was an important landmark; the clouds were his weather signs, more reliable than any television forecast; the birds told him if the winter would be hard or mild, the geese return-ing very late when the winter was due to be bad, the swallows flying off early, the bushes thickly berried and missel-thrush and fieldfare and long-tailed tits appearing at the bird tables.

This year would be the year that Flash was born and little else was of importance. He dreaded the years of age in the beasts he tended, the knowledge that their time was short and that he would lose them. He rejoiced at the birth of each new animal on the farm and hated the days of the lambing sales, ill tempered and testy, snapping at Andrew who felt equally torn and snarled back, furious with Tom for caring, and making his misery even greater. All that work, and the young beasts running to end on a pantry shelf . . . people were crazy, Tom often thought and he was probably madder than most.

He revealed some of these thoughts to Sheena, who had never considered such things before. She began to look at clouds, and she and Geordie soon were knowledgeable about wind streamers, and could recognise thunderheads and see the great anvil shapes building up on the moun-tains that brooded beyond the loch.

54

Christmas came and went, a break in routine, a long holiday which gave Geordie time to play with his pup, wild games now, with a rope to pull at in an endless tug-of-war, or a battered old ball which Flash commandeered and raced away with, refusing to bring it back, standing watching the boy, his eyes wicked, his body carefully poised, ready to run as soon as Geordie had almost caught up with him.

Sheena bought a collar and a lead, and a plate for the dog. Tom made a box on legs so that the pup could sleep out of the draughts, and Andrew sent a case of tinned dog food, knowing that Sheena was finding things tight. There was still no news from the lawyers about the settlement of Geordie's parents' affairs or about the compensation for the road crash, which the insurance firm were settling with the lorry driver's insurance firm.

Andrew began to call in with gifts of potatoes and Tom, who bred fancy bantams and sold them for extra money, brought bantam eggs; Andrew began to find he had a surplus of vegetables he couldn't use, having dug more than he needed and got tired of the parsnips, or picked too many sprouts. Sheena knew he was helping and saving her face, but was grateful. Geordie had grown out of all his clothes and been re-fitted, using some of the money from her tiny savings. It frightened her to see her small capital vanish. Suppose the money never came?

The house where Geordie had lived was still unsold. That alone was a worry as it would deteriorate and be worth less as the months went by. Worry kept her awake at night; she was glad to get up each morning and be greeted by the vociferous pup, racing towards her, his tail wagging frantically, his mouth open in goodwill, his brown eyes welcoming her. She could not remember when they had changed colour; they were expressive eyes, showing his misery when Geordie left for school so that Flash lay disconsolate, watching Sheena move about the house, his face forlorn. She was only second best.

55

Geordie was all important. The boy's homecoming caused a wild greeting, and the pup had to be put to wait in the garden, otherwise he behaved like a greyhound, so excited that he hurtled joyously round the house, upstairs, downstairs, across the beds, and over the furniture, unable to contain his delight at seeing his master again.

He was very small. Sometimes Geordie worried about this, and wondered if it meant the dog was sickly, but Flash showed no signs of ailing. He had a good appetite, and also, if not watched, an inclination to steal. He could jump on to a chair and take the meat from the plate on the table, and vanish before anyone had time to realise what had happened.

The boy learned that the dog could out-think him, out-wit him and outrun him.

And then Flash discovered sheep.

Geordie was standing beside Andrew, who had brought the first lambs down from the hills, as Tom expected snow in the next few days. The clouds had a lowering darkness with a sulphur glow between them, and they grouped low on the flanks of the mountains.

Flash saw two ewes, and began to stalk. Slow, slow, down. Slow, slow, down. Geordie was about to call the pup when Andrew put a finger to his lips. Suppose the pup jumped the sheep or worried them? Geordie need not have bothered. Andrew had recognised at once that Flash was a born sheepdog; he moved carefully, without training, and only at the last did excitement master him so that he panicked the sheep and they bolted to the other end of the field.

The dog returned, his mouth wide open in his greeting grin, pride at his own achievement mastering every other feeling.

'He'll make a grand dog,' Andrew said. 'But I wish he were not quite so small. He looks as if we've tried to breed a miniature. I don't know if it was his bad start or Megan's age.'

Megan, hearing her name, wagged her tail. She enjoyed Geordie's visits and greeted Flash gaily, though she was now becoming stiff, and could not race against him as she had raced with her other pups. Andrew watched the signs of age anxiously.

'I'll need to start another dog,' he said regretfully. 'Megan's in fine shape, but she won't last for ever.'

Geordie was afraid that Andrew might want Flash back, but Tom reassured him.

'He has his eye on one of the pups from Whizz, the big sheepdog over at Dallas farm beyond Dundee, on the other side of the country,' Tom said. 'Whizz has done very well at the trials and his pups are in great demand. He goes back to Sirrah, the greatest sheepdog of them all, that belonged to the Ettrick shepherd, the man who wrote poetry.'

'Did he write anything about a sheepdog?' Geordie asked. He loved poetry. The twins had given him a collection of cat poems for Christmas. Their father had given him a selection of Scottish ballads, ranging from 'Lord Ullin's Daughter' to 'Lochinvar'. They caught his imagination and fired it with wonderful stories of rousing deeds, couched in colourful language.

Sometimes at night, Sheena sang. She had once enjoyed singing but somewhere, during her life, the pleasure had been mislaid. Now it was returning. Geordie loved the songs of the Isles; and often sang them himself.

He loved Skye, and the Skye Boat Song. Andrew had taken him to Mallaig one day, along the broad new road that ran beside blue lochs fringed with pure white sand, with the trees dark and green around them, and the brooding islands where ruined castles reminded them both of the old tales of Scotland.

Tom's favourite reading was the book of the Brown Seer, and he too told stories from the past; stories of haunted moors, of places where only the deer dared run, of women waiting for their lovers, lost in the long ago wars; and he recited the Flowers of the Forest, which made Geordie feel both sad and excited all at once.

He read it to Sheena one late afternoon, when the snow lay deep outside and they could not visit Andrew, and she sang to him, her voice soft in the firelit room, while he sat on the hearthrug with Trippie curled against him, rolling to the blaze, and Flash lying, as always, with his head on Geordie's knee, watching the boy's face. Flames flickered on the polished furniture; wood flared and crackled and fell into a soft red ash, and Geordie saw soldiers in the fire; saw men marching; heard the echoes of the battle skirl of pipes, and the soft keening of the women.

'Where have all the huntsmen gone?'

The words were an echo of another time; another world, a world before the motor car, before the aeroplane, before the days of bombs and machine guns, when men fought with swords, and no one could bridge the gap between countries in a few short hours.

'When will they ever learn?'

Sheena's voice stopped. Geordie looked up at his grandmother. She was lying back against the cushions, fighting for breath.

'Grandy!'

Slowly, her colour returned. Geordie switched on the light and looked at his grandmother helplessly. She was far from well.

'I think I have flu,' she said. 'Geordie, can you ring the doctor, lad?'

He went to the phone, but the line was down and the instrument was dead.

He opened the front door.

There were no landmarks. The mountains were giant bulks of white against the sky; the road had vanished; the path had gone; only in the far distance was the shapeless lump that was Andrew's farmhouse with dirty smoke pluming from the chimney, spiralling into the sky.

He went back into the room.

Sheena was lying against the cushions, her eyes closed. Fear became terror. Geordie fetched blankets from her bed to cover her; filled the hot water bags and put them against her; banked up the fire and put the guard against it.

He would have to go out into the snow. Would have to try and reach Andrew, and Tom would have to fetch the doctor. He couldn't leave her like that; not all night. And there might be more snow before morning.

He tried to remember all that Tom had told him about snow in the past; about the dangers of lying in a drift, till the thaw came; about the dangers of getting lost; of finding no landmarks; of falling through into the ditch.

He went back to look at his grandmother.

Her eyes were closed and she was breathing heavily.

He had no choice.

He put Trippie in the dining-room, and switched on the fire for her. He was afraid she might jump on his grandmother. He checked the fireguard and the blankets and moved the hot water bags. He was desperately afraid.

Suppose Grandy was dying?

Suppose she died while he was looking for help?

Suppose she recovered and found him gone?

He tried hard to think.

He found a pen and wrote a note which he put on the table beside her.

I have gone to tell Tom to get the doctor.
                              Love,
                                        Geordie.
P.S. Don't worry. I'll be all right.

He fetched Flash's lead and fastened it. He would have to carry the dog. The pup would never be able to walk in all that snow.

Wellingtons.

An extra jersey and his warm lined anorak and his

woolly hat and thick gloves. Thick socks.

Food. Never go out in snow without food, Tom had said. Good old Faceache. He taught without even trying.

Raisins. That's what explorers took. And chocolate. There were two bars in the pantry. He was supposed to make them last all week, but this was an emergency. And he hadn't had his supper. Grandy had intended to cook it later. Cheese. That would be useful. And three bread rolls.

He bit into one of them. It was stale but he was hungry.

He lifted Flash and then remembered he would need a key. He had to take it from his grandmother's handbag and felt guilty as he did so, rummaging among her private possessions. There was a wallet inside the bag, beside the key ring. It dropped on the floor as he searched, falling open to reveal the pictures of his mother and father on their wedding day, and of the two of them at his christening, himself in a long dress and shawl, his mother holding him, smiling up at his father.

He closed the wallet hastily, and put the keys safely in his pocket, buttoning it up tight so that if he fell they would not vanish under the snow.

It was all up to him.

His grandmother had not moved.

The door closing behind him felt unpleasantly final. He had taken his grandfather's dog-headed walking stick from the umbrella stand, again feeling as if he were stealing; his grandmother did not like it moved. But he must be able to feel his way or he might end up in a drift and neither Andrew nor Tom would look for him; they had no idea he was out.

If only he could light a bonfire and send smoke signals but they would merely think he was playing some new game of his own, or perhaps having an untimely winter barbecue.

The thoughts milled in his head as he looked out at the white waste, and remembered an old film he had seen of

Charlie Chaplin wandering desperately through the snow for days, ending up starving in a little hut with a miner who was hunting for gold and was delirious with hunger.

Geordie bit into the cheese, and stepped into the snow.

He had forgotten that there were two steps and both he and the pup fell sprawling. The pup, meeting snow for the first time, sniffed it, and regaining his feet, began to dig.

'Come on, Flash,' Geordie said impatiently.

He lifted the dog, and set out again, step by careful step, feeling his way to the garden gate. It was impossible to open. He climbed over, losing a wellington in the process.

Panic overtook him.

He had been ages already and he must hurry.

He began to run, stumbling down the lane, forgetting the stick, longing for Andrew or Tom to appear, for some human being to break the lonely landscape, for the air to warm and the snow to vanish by magic. It was bitterly cold and his ears ached and his face hurt, and the stinging wind spoke of more snow to come, bringing with it a few huge clinging wet flakes that fell on the dog's head, so that he shook himself vigorously.

Geordie struggled on.

The farmhouse was within sight, and he forgot caution, stepping to one side of the path.

The snow gave way and he fell, floundering in a drift. He could see nothing. Struggling only sent him deeper.

And, worst of all, he had dropped his dog.

Snow filled his mouth and his eyes and his ears. He landed with a bump, in a dug out cave in which were three sheep, huddled together, that Andrew had failed to find. He cuddled down between them, clearing his mouth and eyes, and they stayed, patient, accepting him as a companion in misfortune.

Geordie tried to fight his way out of the drift, but snow fell in on him, and collapsed around him. He was better staying quite still with the sheep for warmth. He crept between them again and nibbled at one of the bars of chocolate. He wondered how long he could live if he rationed himself carefully and sucked the snow for water. No one would be looking for him.

His grandmother might be dead and now he had every chance of dying too.

And Flash had no chance at all, a tiny dog, alone in the snow, not knowing how to survive, not able to walk.

Tears began to trickle down Geordie's cheeks and nothing he could do would stop them.

Chapter Four

Flash had been born determined. He had fought for life at birth; had fought for it as Geordie reared him, in spite of the abscess at only two days old; he never gave up once he had made up his small mind.

He fell on hard-packed snow when Geordie dropped him, and stood, and shook himself, bewildered by the disappearance of his master.

The world was very strange and very large. Flash nosed the snow. It held no scent that he could recognise. There had been birds across it, and there was the snowshoe track of a rabbit, that he followed to the middle of the lane, and then forgot, feeling cold and hungry and lonely. It had been almost time for his feed when Geordie left the house, and he had not brought even a biscuit for the dog, thinking he would reach the farmhouse safely. The food had been an insurance, an 'if I take it with me, I won't need it; nothing will go wrong'.

A bird flew overhead, casting a stark shadow. The pup sat and watched it, his ears angled, curious. He chased the shadow for a moment, nosing it, but it had no smell and he paused, one leg bent, thoughtful, puzzling this strange appearance. He became aware of his own shadow, flung before by the sun. He moved and the dark shape moved. He pricked his ears and the shadow ears pricked up.

His paws were freezing.

He whimpered with pain, and nosed around the drift, aware that Geordie was there, able to scent both the boy and the sheep. The pup dug, but digging was futile. The drift was far too deep for his small paws.

Over at the farmhouse, Andrew was carrying hay for the sheep in the byres. He had moved the cattle into the big barn, and packed the sheep into their place. The work was endless; a constant bringing in of hay, and a constant mucking out. He slipped on a patch of ice, fell headlong, and yelled in fury.

Tom was throwing bales of hay from the top of the stack to the ground. He called out.

'Are you all right?'

The familiar voice sounded along the lane, and the pup set off to find it. He knew Tom well. Tom had been helping Geordie teach the pup his first manners; to sit and stay and go down; to walk at heel, and to come when called. One day Tom would teach the boy how to work the sheep. Flash had potential for all his small size.

The snow was hard packed, from the constant passage of sheep. Tom and Andrew and Megan had been working all day, thrusting crooks into the drifts, bringing out stranded animals and driving them home. It was a hard grind. Snow was always a penance, here under the mountains.

The pup plodded on, aware of the sting of cold in his eyes, and the bitter numbing cold beneath his paws. Snowflakes clung to his thick fur. He shook his head, hating the drifting wetness. There was more snow in the sky; snow in the heavy sagging clouds; snow forecast by the lurid light.

There was a sudden crack as the sky forked into lightning, and the clouds bellowed their rage.

The pup ran. He had never heard thunder before and he was terrified. He whimpered loudly.

Megan heard him and began to bark.

'For Heaven's sake,' Andrew said irritably. 'What in the world is wrong with that bitch?'

She was running to and fro across the farmyard, barking at them, chasing frantically between Tom and Andrew, frustrated beyond measure at their stupidity. She was telling them, as plainly as she could, that her pup was out there, in the snow, crying for her, and she needed the gate opened so that she could go to him.

'Quiet, Megan,' Andrew ordered.

The bitch raced to Tom and barked again.

'Maybe there's a fox out there,' Tom said, walking to the gate and peering down the lane.

He stared in disbelief at the tiny black and white pup walking wearily along in the distance, his lead dragging.

'Holy Joe! It's the pup! What in the world . . .?' Tom opened the gate and Megan ran down the lane, over the hard-packed snow, and nosed Flash. He greeted her rapturously. Tom, reaching the two dogs, bent to lift the pup, but Flash turned and began to plod back towards the drift. Geordie was there, only he couldn't reach him. When the man bent down again, the pup lifted his head and howled.

'Dear Heaven,' Andrew said, as he heard, and came running down the lane with his crook.

'Surely the boy wouldn't have come in this snow?' Andrew said.

Tom was looking at the wires lying on the ground, and the deep footprints leading along the lane from the cottage gate.

'The phone would be out of action; and Sheena Graham's no kitten,' he said.

He put the pup back on the ground.

Flash set off again, nosing his own trail, until he came to the piled-up snow, where he began once more to dig. Tom had brought his spade, picking it up automatically as he left the farmyard, in case Megan found more stranded sheep. She had an excellent nose for buried animals. She was digging now, barking, small shrill excited barks as the snow flew behind her frantic legs.

Tom shovelled snow as if a life depended on it, as indeed it might. He grunted when he caught a glimpse of red that was Geordie's anorak and dug more carefully, flinging the snow behind him. Andrew joined him, using his hands to throw out the snow, pushing it away so that it would not fall into the gully Tom had made.

Geordie stared up at them, lying between the sheep.

'Lad, lad, are you all right?' Tom's face was as anxious as his voice.

'I haven't been here long,' Geordie said. 'Grandy's ill; very ill, and the phone's dead.'

'Are you fit to walk home?' Andrew asked.

Geordie nodded.

'Tom can take the Land-Rover to the village; we've cleared the path our side to the road and were coming up to you later; the snow plough has proved its worth today. The main road's clear; they've been working on it all day. We'll get back and see what we can do,' Andrew said.

Geordie was glad to move again; he stank of sheep. Megan and Tom drove the sheep home, and into the byres. Tom shut the doors on the animals, and took the bitch with him to drive into the village. Their own phone was dead too.

Sheena had not moved.

Andrew looked at her, knowing this was more than flu; a heart attack, or a stroke maybe; she was a bad colour and breathing with difficulty. He sent Geordie to fill the hot water bags again, and to feed the pup, while he himself added an extra blanket and stoked the fire, and cursed the snow.

Geordie came back into the room. The pup came to the fire to warm himself but the return of life to his frozen paws was painful and he whimpered unhappily.

'Move him from the heat and rub his paws,' Andrew said. 'Gently, with a warm towel. You know what it's like when your hands come back to life again after being cold. Are you dry, lad?'

Geordie shook his head.

'Then go and have a warm bath as soon as the pup's warm, and put on dry clothes.' Andrew was glad to be able to think of a natural occupation that would take the boy out of the room. He was afraid Sheena would die before the doctor arrived.

Flash followed Geordie upstairs and curled down on the bathmat beside the warm bath. He was not letting Geordie out of his sight again. The terror at finding himself alone in the snow would remain for the whole of his life. He stood up once, paws on the edge of the bath, and licked at Geordie's hair.

Geordie, feeling the water warm him, feeling the numbness leaving his own hands and feet, was too worried about his grandmother to notice the pain in his fingers and toes. He was sure Grandy would have to go to hospital; and what about him? Where would he go? Perhaps Andrew would give him a bed and he could help on the farm; he didn't want to stay in the cottage, all alone. The houses were scattered and the farm was their nearest neighbour, almost a quarter of a mile away, although they could see it plainly, as Grandy's cottage was on the hill, and the farmhouse lay below it, towards the distant loch.

Fear kept Geordie in the bath, topping up the hot water. He could not bear to remember his grandmother's face; could not bear to see her helpless; to face the fact that she might die. She was old; so old, and she was always tired and a little out of breath by evening. And he did make a lot of work.

If only his parents hadn't been killed. If only he were older. His lame leg ached. They should have gone to the hospital the next day, but that was out of the question. If only life went smoothly, day following day as it had when he was small, and everything seemed to happen with unbroken regularity; meals and bed; and getting up again, and his mother calling to him to hurry or he'd be late for school; the weekends with his father and football in the garden. Now he couldn't play football at all; perhaps he would never play again. He couldn't run fast and his leg sometimes felt as if it were made of lead and not of flesh and bone.

He envied Flash, who could run without difficulty. It must be wonderful to be a dog; a dog in a good home, fed and exercised, and with no knowledge of the world; or of the need to work and earn money and to survive. How did you survive with no one at all belonging to you, Geordie wondered, as he towelled himself dry. There was only his mother's cousin, Jennie Anderson, in Manchester. She was a teacher and had visited them when he was small. But he couldn't remember her.

Fear settled heavily on Geordie as he dressed. The doorbell rang while he was combing his hair and he heard the doctor's voice. Then there was a long terrifying silence.

Was Grandy dead?

He dared not go downstairs.

He sat on the top stair, shivering, with the dog held tightly against him as if the pup could keep the troubles of the world at a distance.

There was snow on the windowsill, and the sky was dark. Large flakes drifted out of the sky and settled on the pane.

If there are three flakes before I count three Grandy will be all right, Geordie thought. He counted. One, Two, Three. There were four flakes. Did that count, or did it upset the omen? He needed an omen. He needed reassurance. He needed someone to come and hug him and tell him it didn't matter; it would be all right; it wouldn't hurt tomorrow.

He buried his face in the pup's warm fur and sat quite still.

Thought was as terrifying as reality; perhaps more so. He had to blank out his mind.

Oh young Lochinvar is come out of the West,
Through all the wide border his steed was the best . . .

He couldn't remember the words properly. He must think of something he could remember, all the way through and say it over and over again.

'Come back, come back,' he cried in grief,
Across the stormy water.
'And I'll forgive your Highland chief,
My daughter, oh my daughter.'

That wasn't very cheering either. He tried Lord
Randal, but neither was dying of poison a particularly
comforting idea. Nobody ever lived happily; fairy tales
were just for babies, to make them sleep at night. Geordie
was old and grown up, and he was totally alone. Nobody
cared. There was nobody else in the world who'd want
him and he'd have to go into a Home. He imagined it, as
cold and bare and bleak as the Home that Oliver Twist
went to; a place of bullying boys and harsh adults and
not enough to eat.

He hadn't realised how hungry he was. If only there
was some of Grandy's Scotch broth left; or a plate full of
roast meat and baked potatoes.

'Geordie,' Andrew looked up, half guessing at the boy's
state of mind. 'Your grandmother will have to go to
hospital for a little while. You can come home with me.
It will be nice to have company for a change. Go and
pack yourself a bag of all you need, and find Trippie's
carrying basket; and the doctor wants to look at you. Just
to make sure you are all right after being in that drift.'

Geordie did not ask the question lying on his tongue.
Will she be all right? Andrew had given him no reassurance. Andrew never did tell him fairy tales. He had
said that Jesskin would die when the goat had milk fever
and she had died; and he had said that Lady, the big bay
mare, would have to be shot as she had a stomach cancer,
though Grandy had thought it better the boy shouldn't
know about the shooting and should think the mare had
died naturally.

His pyjamas were folded neatly under his pillow. He
packed his case, wishing someone could do it for him as
nothing lay flat. Shirts and pants and socks and jerseys;

69

toothbrush; his four favourite books; and lastly, hidden under all the clothes, his old teddy bear.

When he went downstairs there was an ambulance man at the gate, and a second bringing a stretcher. He watched as they wrapped Grandy up in blankets, tucking in hot water bags on either side of her, pulling up the covers to protect her face. Was she dead?

Then her eyes opened and she saw Geordie and tried to smile. 'Be a good boy,' she whispered.

The doctor followed them.

'He'll be back to look at you,' Andrew said. He was busying himself, making the fire safe, poking the logs flat, ensuring that the guard was in place. He went upstairs to turn the water off, and to drain the tank.

'I'll get Tom to come in every day and put the electric fires on for a while and keep the place warm for you to come back to,' Andrew said.

'Will I come back?' Geordie asked.

'I don't know,' Andrew said at last. 'We don't know how bad your grandmother is. A lot depends on how quickly they can get her to hospital. It's going to be rough travelling.'

'How will they get her there?' Geordie asked. Glasgow was a three-hour journey in the best of weather.

'By helicopter. It won't take long,' Andrew answered. 'Now wash Flash's plate and find his food; and Trippie's; better not to change their diet or we'll have two upset little beasts on our hands and there's enough work to do.'

'I can help,' Geordie said quickly, terrified lest he too was extra work.

'I know that,' Andrew answered, and squeezed the boy's shoulder wishing he could provide more comfort, wishing the boy had some hope of some childhood; he was being forced into adulthood far too soon. He was a solemn little grommet. Andrew sighed. Life wasn't much fun; never had been perhaps. War and quake and famine; you salvaged what you could and built yourself a cocoon of security which you tried to keep intact. Who was it wrote of the arrows of outrageous fortune? Geordie had had enough of them flung at him.

The snow began again that afternoon. Snow fell all night and all of the next day and Tom could not get back to his own home. They shovelled desperately in the yard, keeping the path free to feed the beasts and clean them out. Geordie worked with the men; carrying and fetching hay; moving among the animals; his ears, like theirs, listening for sounds of trouble. One of the ewes died in the night, delivering a stillborn premature lamb. Geordie found them both in the morning.

There was no news at all. No papers. No telephone. The radio was their only link with the world outside and that carried stories of farms like theirs, of animals stranded on the moors; of hay dropped by helicopter for the deer and the ponies.

Andrew was well stocked. The deep freeze was full and Tom was a good bread maker; they ate hot buttered rolls at tea time, by a blazing fire, while the dogs stretched out in front of the flames; and then Tom cooked mountains of ham and eggs, and brought out frozen fruit which he made into pies and served with custard so thick the spoon stood up in it.

Geordie could not go to school; he could not venture into the world outside. Time seemed to stand still; day followed day, with a sameness that was unchanging; the needs of the beasts and their own needs; the need to shovel the snow that fell nightly.

Each morning the world was white again; the mountains shimmered in the thin winter sunshine; the loch was gone, a span of ice covered over by snow. Fields and woods and lanes and roads had vanished. Nothing moved outside except for a fox that ran along a track which was plainly the top of a field wall, dragging a hare in its jaws.

Night after night Geordie lay, watching the sky, watching the snow, wondering about his grandmother.

71

Was she alive? Had she died? And if not would she be well enough to come home again and look after him? Or was it his fault she was ill, making too much work?

He did not know.

The pup slept on his bed and though Andrew disapproved of dogs in bedrooms he recognised the boy's need and allowed Flash to follow Geordie upstairs. The dog and the boy were inseparable. Flash was a shadow, always at heel, following among the sheep, as gentle with them as Megan, who showed him how to behave, and snapped quickly at his small nose if he were too boisterous.

Flash slept in the crook of Geordie's arm, with his head on the boy's shoulder. It was a comfort in the night to know the little animal was there, with his warm body and his soft ears; to see him sit up and stare at the moon; to feel the cold nose slide into a warm hand; and to hear the soft breathing. It eased the loneliness, which was something that neither Tom nor Andrew could do.

By day Geordie was quiet; too quiet. Doing as he was told; helping out with the air of someone twice his age so that it was hard for both men to realise he was only just turned eleven. He had forgotten childhood. He accepted death in the animals now. Another lamb had died, born too close to the door, freezing, with the birth water still wet on its wool. The ewe left it and stood bereft refusing to eat. Geordie had not realised that animals mourned.

He laid the table; cut the bread; washed the dishes; fetched the eggs; listened quietly to the news; looked out over the white desolation. Sometimes Tom talked about other snowings; about the night he had been out on his pony, and lost in the woods; and he recited Robert Frost's poem:

> But I have promises to keep
> And miles to go before I sleep.

Geordie could imagine the man and his pony in the deep woods, staring at the winter beauty. It was very beautiful although it meant death to so many creatures.

'Christmas card weather, out of season,' Tom said one morning, watching Flash, who adored snow, and played with it, scuffing it up behind him; leaping and rolling in it, nosing in it.

Tom rolled a snowball and threw it at Geordie.

Geordie stared and then retaliated and a moment later Andrew joined in, until the yard was splattered with burst snowballs and the dogs were leaping in an ecstasy of merriment, trying to catch them, shaking their heads when they exploded into a flurry of flakes instead of staying whole.

Geordie laughed.

It was the first time he had laughed for days and Andrew resolved that they would think more often of the needs of a boy. And it didn't hurt them to relax. They worked the better afterwards, and Tom whistled cheerfully as he tedded hay, and cleaned out the stable while Smoke, the grey mare, watched thoughtfully, and nuzzled Geordie when he brought her carrots.

That night Tom brought out one of Andrew's books and began to read aloud before bedtime. There was peace in the quiet room. Geordie loved the big kitchen, the tiled floor, the rag rugs, the wicker chairs that creaked as you moved, the cushions that Andrew's wife had made, the big dresser with plates and cups and saucers and the prize cards won at shows by the animals. None were recent; life had become too busy since Elspeth had died.

The fire blazed; Geordie lay on the rug, Megan at his feet, Flash at his side, and listened to Tom's deep voice. It was a story he knew well, the story of a boy and a dog, in another time, another country; it was a happy story, so that when he went to bed that night he felt new hope. Grandy would get well again and he'd be able to look after her. He was grown up now and had learned so much with Andrew.

Geordie began to think the snow would never go. The

mornings were bright, the sun sparkling on whiteness. Tom made him a toboggan and he took Flash and slid down the slope in the field; but he felt it wrong to enjoy himself when his grandmother might be dead. No one could get through to them.

They were cut off from everywhere, the lane so deep with snow that it was impossible to know which was road and which was hedge. Those sheep left out on the hills would certainly be dead. Once a helicopter flew over, and dropped bales of hay and a sack of food. Tins of meat and fruit; potato powder in packets, causing Tom to exclaim in disgust although he was glad enough to eat it. They had not been able to reach the clamps. The fields were too dangerous; the drifts too deep.

There was chocolate as well, and dried milk, which amused Andrew, as they were pouring milk into all the animals, unable to deliver it. They only had four milkers but usually they provided their neighbours. Queenie's latest litter grew fat on fresh milk and the cats enjoyed themselves too, unrationed.

Tom took Geordie into the big barn every day to show him how to train his dog. Flash enjoyed working, moving swiftly at heel, his eyes on Geordie's face. He moved so fast at times that Geordie had to train him off the lead, making the dog walk slowly, keep to heel, and not outpace him.

Flash hated staying; he hated Geordie moving away from him, leaving him isolated, and time after time he followed. Again and again Geordie put him back, stood beside him, reassuring him, making him stay still. When he called the dog to him, Flash came so fast that he almost overbalanced as he braked.

'He'll do,' Tom said, after one session, as the dog came to Geordie for praise, knowing he had done well. His tail waved enthusiastically. It was late February and he was almost four months old. They had been snowed up for over a month. The pup was young for training but the boy needed distraction. Short lessons did not harm.

Maybe the mail would come by helicopter, Tom said one morning, but nothing came. They watched the sky, and longed for contact with other people.

There was little they could do about the farm. Andrew taught Geordie to play double handed patience, a game he had often played with his wife, and Tom, who carried a box of poker dice with him, taught the boy to play poker dice; using matches to represent one thousand pounds each. By the time Geordie had lost £20,000 to Tom he had learned not to play poker for money.

The needs of the sheep and the animals dominated everything else. There was food enough; and time to cook it. Tom found an old recipe book and began to make new dishes; Fat Rascals for tea became Geordie's favourite; little scone-like cakes dripping with butter as they were eaten hot. He began to learn to cook, with Tom and Andrew encouraging him to try more ambitious food than bacon and eggs.

Time ceased to have any meaning when there was no school, although it was term time. There would be no children in the village school, as every farm would be isolated and no children lived in the village itself.

The day began when the sun rose, and ended with sunset. The sun was low in the sky with little warmth and the nights were freezing. Flash began to explore the barns, nosing the sheep, visiting the mare, staring up at the cows, who plumed their scented breath at him, and nosed him in turn, curious.

He raced into the biggest barn one morning after Chitty, the ginger cat that hated dogs and fled from them. Flash was in need of exercise. His small body was alive with joy, and he could not resist the cat. He misjudged his distance and shot between the stored sacks of fertiliser, ready for winter, and disturbed a half-grown vixen that had come into shelter.

She leaped at him, her vicious teeth raking his ear and his jaw. He yelped and bit her shoulder, and as he leaped

75

clear she caught his paw and held on. Tom heard the din and ran, and seized the broom, slamming the handle down on the vixen's nose. She yelped, and fled, through the barn and across the yard, and leaping the wall, was buried in a drift.

Geordie lifted his pup. The ear was torn; the jaw had been badly bitten, a gash of open flesh where the teeth had raked his lip, but the paw was worst of all. The teeth had met and held and the pup could not bear any weight on the leg. He limped as soon as he was put on the ground, holding the injured paw high.

Tom took him indoors, and bathed the injuries. He looked out at the snow; at the sullen sky; at the distance that separated them from Angus; at the useless telephone. There was penicillin ointment in the stable, which they had used on the cow. It would perhaps help, but the pup needed an injection, right now, and they had nothing at all they could give him. And though Andrew had a hypodermic for the cattle and knew how to use it, he hadn't got one small enough for a dog.

That night, when Geordie had gone to bed, the pup did not follow him. He lay by the fire, shivering.

'And what do we do about that?' Tom asked, wishing he knew how to ski, or had snowshoes.

'What can we do?' Andrew asked.

Neither voiced the thoughts in his mind.

By daylight the pup had no desire to move. He lay on the hearthrug, and Geordie had to force glucose and water into him. He refused all food. Tom knew the small animal had a high temperature; he looked through their medicine box, and found nothing at all that was safe for a young dog. They could only keep the pup warm, and hope that his resistance was strong enough to let him recover without veterinary help.

There was no chance whatever of that.

The torn ear and the gash on the pup's face began to heal cleanly.

The pup would have a twisted lip, as the wound was going to scar. Tom had stitched it, but he was not as expert as Angus with a needle although he was always able to stitch an injured cow or pig, or put in the few stitches needed to stop the calf bed from coming out of the cow after a difficult delivery.

The paw festered.

Tom poulticed the injury; he lanced the wound; but the poison was deeper than the surface; and he was afraid that it would spread through the pup's whole system. If only he could at least phone Angus and find out what he could do; or if there were anything he could do. If only he had known the vixen was there. But it was no use worrying about what was done.

Geordie worked with the men, without speaking, running back frequently to look at the pup, now a very sick animal indeed. He would eat, a very little, so long as Geordie fed him with his fingers. Tom cooked a chicken and they shredded the flesh; they took bones from the deep freeze and made quantities of broth, which the pup drank; he limped out of doors, very briefly, and came in again, and Andrew was afraid the cold would chill him.

At night he lay against Megan and wanted nothing to do with Geordie. He could not even mount the stairs, and Tom thought it best that he should not be carried. A sick dog in the bedroom was most unwise.

Tom came downstairs on the second day of March to find that Andrew had remembered it was his birthday. Breakfast was cooked; and there were two small parcels on the table. One contained a bookmark, made from cardboard, decorated with tiny matchstick animals, with Tom's name written on it, and a coloured cord threaded through it. The label read: TO FACEACHE. HAPPY BIRTH-DAY. GEORDIE. The other contained a pair of socks that Andrew had bought and never worn, and a birthday card made from half of a Christmas card.

'I'll do better when it thaws,' Andrew said.

Geordie had iced a cake; making whorls and squiggles; and as they cut into it, Geordie was aware of an unusual sound.

'Listen,' Tom said.

There was a slither and a scurry. Megan barked and the pup lifted his head to listen. There was a crash and the windows darkened as there was another sliding noise.

'It's thawing,' Tom said. 'That's the best present I could have had.'

He looked at the pup. Flash had eaten almost nothing that day. His small body was starvation thin; his coat stared, and his eyes were dull. The bitch nosed him and licked him, as if determined to keep him alive.

There were dripping noises from outside.

The thaw had come suddenly. Perhaps if they were lucky, they would be able to get through to the village; would be able to get help from Angus; be able to have news of Sheena.

Geordie was sitting on the hearthrug, his cake untouched on the plate beside him. His hands continually stroked the pup's fur. Flash licked a finger, but his tail only moved in a token thump.

Geordie needed an omen.

If Tom picked up a knife; or if Andrew took a bite of his cake.

It was a silly omen. Andrew picked up the knife and cut another slice of cake and Tom bit into his with satisfaction.

'Eat up, Geordie lad. Snow'll be gone by morning and we'll get Flash to Angus somehow,' Tom said.

Geordie could not eat the cake. The mere thought choked him.

He knew that they wouldn't be in time.

Chapter Five

The thaw continued.

By the second day the road was passable.

The telephone lines were not yet repaired, but by ten o'clock the snow plough had arrived, and Tom sent an urgent message to Angus, who came at lunchtime, having been able to leave his own home for the first time for days. He had driven into the village by the long route round the mountain in order to hold an emergency surgery for animals he had been unable to treat.

The vet came into the room, his face sombre, and handed a note to Andrew, who read it, and put it in his pocket. Geordie, aware of a change in atmosphere, thought it was because his pup was going to die. He knelt beside Flash, who, that morning, had not even wagged his tail. He was a small, sick, sorry little beast, the gashes on his head half healed, the bite on his paw a swollen mass that nothing had been able to ease.

Andrew had bathed it daily; had put fomentations on the paw; had tried all he knew to draw the pus, but the vixen had bitten deep and the infection was now widespread.

Angus examined the paw, his face revealing none of his thoughts. There was little hope; little chance, but with the news that lay in Andrew's pocket, he had to do something, had to hope against hope, had to try and save the little dog. He was afraid of gangrene; an ever present danger with animal injuries of this kind.

'I can't promise, Geordie,' he said. 'I'll do what I can. All I can.'

Flash did not even lift his head when the needle went in. He was in a lonely world of intense pain. His temperature

79

had soared; and he was aware of little that went on around him. The smell of Geordie, and the knowledge of Geordie there beside him, was comfort, and the pup did his best to take the glucose and water dripped into his mouth, but he had to be made to swallow. He was very close to death.

'Keep him warm, and I'll be back this evening,' Angus said. There was news for Geordie and he did not want to be there when it was told. He was too soft-hearted. He did not envy Andrew his task.

Tom had been down to the village with the snow plough and come back with a large supply of fresh bones. He started to make bone broth in the pressure cooker.

'Bone broth works wonders,' Tom said. 'I've known it bring a child back from near death; never mind a pup.'

Geordie would not leave the hearthrug. Andrew watched him, wishing he could reach the boy, who had become almost unaware of the two men. His whole concentration was on Flash, willing him to live, willing him to get better, willing him to take notice. Andrew had little hope. And the note in his pocket burned into his mind. Somehow, he had to tell Geordie that his grandmother had died while they were snowed up, and been buried, and that the boy was to go to his mother's cousin, Jennie, in Manchester. He couldn't tell him now. Wait and see what happened to the pup.

At lunchtime Geordie barely ate, though Tom had cooked all his favourite food. Neither man knew what to say to the boy; neither man had any consolation to offer. There were some things that no amount of consolation could ease. Later, in the pig sty, where Queenie was suckling twelve little pigs, Andrew showed Tom the note.

'Better if the dog dies,' Tom said. 'The boy can't take that to Manchester with him. No life for a collie.'

It was a thought that had not occurred to Andrew, who found himself in a dilemma. He didn't want the pup; and who would take it? He hadn't time for an extra dog; he was taking on Whizz's son as soon as the snow cleared and would be very busy training the newcomer. An untrained pup was a danger on the farm with no one to watch over him. Flash would spend his life shut in. Andrew did not care for the thought; and the little dog was no use as yet for herding; it was going to be a headache all right. Even if Flash recovered there was every chance he would be lame.

Worry needled Andrew all day, so that when he came in at tea time he was surly and in no mood to break his news to Geordie.

Angus returned at six.

'I haven't told him,' Andrew said. 'I don't know how; not now. Is that pup going to live?'

Angus shrugged.

'I can't do much more,' he said. 'Another injection. Has it shown any sign of noticing the world today?'

Andrew shook his head. The pup had not moved from the hearthrug; had not even lifted its head to be given the bone broth. Geordie had had to hold him; Flash had not responded to a hand on his fur, not even by the faintest twitch of his tail. Tom was busy with the animals, not able to face the quiet room, where nothing seemed to move except the slowly ticking clock and the shadows cast by the flames.

Geordie had retreated into his own world; a world which terrified him, a world without his dog. The past few months had been the happiest he had known since his parents had died. Flash was consolation; was companionship; was fun; something to play with, to run with, and although Geordie had not realised it, games with the pup had done far more for his lame leg than any amount of physiotherapy. The limp was almost unnoticeable.

The slow evening passed. Tom had gone to his own home. Andrew sat, trying to read the paper, one eye on the boy. Geordie said nothing when spoken to, apparently not hearing. He sat on the rug, the pup's head on his knee, stroking, stroking, stroking. Andrew was almost mesmerised by the moving hand. Twice he tried to speak, to tell Geordie about Sheena's death, but the words would not come.

The coals and the logs hissed and flared. Firelight was reflected in the pup's open eyes. He lay, staring at nothing, no recognition at all of anything around him. He did not move when Megan came to lick him. She curled up beside Geordie and pushed her head against the pup.

The time crept on.

The boy should be in bed, but he wouldn't sleep. He would only fret. Andrew could not bear to send Geordie upstairs, knowing he would lie awake in the darkened room, with the same expression in his eyes as that in the dog's.

Geordie fed the pup with bone broth every hour, on the hour. The drops dripped into Flash's mouth from a tiny eye dropper. So little to keep a dog alive. There was medicine too. Angus had given the pup a second injection, knowing there was little else he could do. The injection would make it sleepy, he warned Geordie.

A coal slipped from the fire, making Andrew and Geordie and Megan jump. Megan growled, not knowing what had made the noise. Andrew hushed her, and she wagged her tail and returned to the boy, lying beside him, again washing the pup's fur, as if he were once more tiny and helpless.

If only they could go back again. If only the vixen hadn't been in the barn. Geordie went outside to warm the broth again. He added the medicine to it; it was easier to give both together.

He lifted the pup's head.

The warm drops fell on the dog's tongue.

There was a flicker in the brown eyes. A moment later, the pup swallowed, by himself, without the need to stroke his throat.

He swallowed a second time, and his tongue licked his chops. Geordie dripped in a third drop, almost holding his breath. Had he imagined it? Had the pup moved? Had his expression changed?

Andrew was watching.

He remembered an old dodge he had used before on animals near to death. He fetched the brandy bottle and poured six drops from it into the saucer of bone broth.

'Try that, lad,' he said.

Geordie re-filled the pipette.

He squeezed the rubber bulb, and the warm brandy-laced broth dripped into the pup's mouth.

He swallowed.

Geordie emptied the pipette.

'Shall I give him more?' he asked.

The small tail wagged at the sound of his master's voice. Only a feeble effort, but a definite movement.

Andrew nodded.

The pup took all the broth in the saucer. Megan washed the sticky lips, and the pup nosed her, and curled against her; this time, he slept.

'He's turned the corner,' Andrew said. 'Bed, lad. I'll watch over him tonight.'

He watched the boy's smile.

'Can I have something to eat, please,' Geordie asked.

Andrew went out into the kitchen to warm milk and to make toast, and knew, as he did so, that he was going to miss the child. He did not want to part with him. If only he and Elspeth had had a child . . .

There was no point in that thought. It was an old thought, and a bitter thought. He had never wanted to marry again; no time for courting and not many women about who would take on the job of a farmer's wife; that needed a special kind of person. But a son . . .

Geordie ate for the first time since the pup had become ill. The pup woke, and wagged his tail when Geordie spoke. He was definitely taking notice again.

'He's getting better,' Geordie said. He bent to hug the pup before going up to bed, and Andrew knew he could not break bad news tonight. The boy needed sleep, and would sleep dreamless now.

The man wondered if Geordie had even thought about his grandmother.

'Sleep well,' he said, as Geordie went towards the door.

The boy paused and looked back at the pup.

'Grandy's dead, isn't she?' he said, and Andrew stared at him, startled.

'How did you know?'

'You'd have said if she'd been all right,' Geordie said. 'And I saw you look at Angus. I just knew.'

He went out of the room, leaving Andrew staring into the fire, pondering the extraordinary mentality of children. Geordie showed no emotion whatever. But perhaps he had exhausted his capacity for feeling in the past few days. He had not even asked where he was to go.

Andrew fed the pup and dosed it again at two o'clock. This time the pup co-operated, taking the broth greedily. It was definitely on the way to recovery. Andrew banked the fire and replaced the guard, leaving Megan to curl herself round Flash and keep him warm.

He went up, wearily, to bed, and undressed swiftly, leaving his clothes on the floor, too exhausted to care. Yet once in bed he could not sleep.

He watched the moon soar between the branches of the trees outside his window; watched the shadows cast across the snow on the mountains, which gleamed in the pale light, towering over the farmhouse, visible even from his bed.

He did not want morning to come.

He did not want to tell Geordie he was to go and live in Manchester.

And he wondered if perhaps he could phone the unknown cousin and ask her to take the dog.

When he slept he dreamed that the dog was dead and Geordie was standing beside him, shaking him in fury.

He woke to find he had overslept and Tom had come to find out what was wrong and was shaking him.

'One of the milkers is down,' Tom said. 'I rang Angus. They've repaired the line. Have you told the boy?'

'I didn't need to. He guessed,' Andrew said, yawning, and wishing he need never get up again.

'The pup's on its feet,' Tom said, as he went out of the room.

Andrew dressed, and went in to see Geordie.

The boy was still sound asleep.

Andrew let him sleep on. It delayed the need to tell bad news, and the lad needed rest. He had spent three nights beside the pup; and heaven alone knew if he would sleep tonight.

Morning was bitingly cold, and Andrew shivered as he walked across the yard.

Tom was talking to Queenie, at the top of his voice, always an ominous sign.

Andrew sighed. He had too much to worry about, without some new grievance of Tom's.

'The man's daft, lass,' Tom was saying, his back expressing all his indignation. He reminded Andrew, improbably, of the haystack cat, Mouser, a vast grey tomcat that could express ardent interest by means of his erect quivering tail, as he watched a rat hole.

'Sending the boy to someone he doesn't even know when he could stay here; when he's grown used to us; where he gets on. He won't settle in Manchester with that fancy cousin. What'll he do in the town? And it'll break him to leave the pup.'

Andrew walked away, refusing to be drawn into argument. It was bad enough to have to tell Geordie; bad enough to part with the boy; he had enjoyed having him around. He grew more irritable as he began the milking. The old machine needed replacing and the pump stopped twice; the cows seemed more than usually awkward, with Mazabel refusing to go into her place, and Jezebel, always evil tempered, lashing out with a hind leg as he passed her. Susabel fouled the stall.

85

By the time milking was done and everything tidied away, and the churns lugged outside to the tractor, Andrew's temper had risen, so that when Tom came up to speak to him he snapped, and Tom walked off, furious in his turn.

Geordie had made breakfast. The table was laid; bacon and eggs in quantity were keeping hot in the oven of the Aga, the bread was cut, and everything was ready. The pup was lapping, drinking bone broth, and when he saw Andrew his tail wagged, a token wag, but at least it was acknowledgement. He stumbled, on three legs, to the door, asking to go out. Geordie took him outside, and carried him in again.

Andrew examined the paw.

The swelling was less; and soon Angus would be here to give another injection. The pup was definitely mending. Andrew looked at the boy. He was eating heartily, watching Flash, who had settled down beside Megan and was looking about him. It was astonishing how quickly an animal could recover.

Tom stumped into the room, and dragged his chair across the floor.

'I'm ready for that; looks good,' he said, and was rewarded by Geordie's vivid smile. Andrew stabbed his fork into a slice of bacon. He couldn't tell the boy; not today. Let him enjoy himself for a while longer. The cousin wouldn't be coming for some time; the road was surely still impassable. They had been cut off for so long.

He would tell the boy tomorrow.

It was a decision he was to regret.

By lunchtime the pup was hungry; Geordie fed him with a spoonful of cooked mince soaked in gravy; and more of the bone broth. He sat on the hearthrug beside the pup, reading, his hand straying constantly to the hard bony head, fondling the soft ears. The pup curled up against the boy, as Megan was missing. He was Geordie's pup again

86

and followed, limping uneasily, when the boy went upstairs. Geordie lifted the pup and carried him.

Geordie sat on the bed in the attic room. It had been Andrew's room when he was a boy, when his parents were alive. Both had died, and Andrew had inherited the farm. It was an old house, more than two hundred years old, Tom said. It cuddled into the hillside. Trees clustered behind it, sheltering it from the prevailing wind.

Geordie loved this room. His room in his grandmother's house had been too feminine, delicate pink on the walls, fragile curtains at the windows, pale pink spread and rug on the creamy carpet, a room made for Grandy's friends, not for him. The dressing-table mirror had been edged with barbola work, clusters of pink and blue flowers massed together at the corners. Even the pictures had been feminine; a wide-eyed small girl holding a kitten; a baby sitting beside a large dog.

This room was totally masculine; the carpet was patterned in brown and gold blocks, the thick bedside rug was dark brown and so was the heavy tweed spread that blended with gold curtains. Andrew's train set was still in one corner of the room, arranged on a large table; Geordie started an engine running; it was a clockwork set, from long ago, but every piece was beautifully made, and it still worked smoothly.

The big chest held Andrew's books from his boyhood. Biggles; and Percy F. Westerman; a battered copy of *Treasure Island*; another of *The Three Musketeers*; most of C. S. Forester. There were school books and an old pair of football boots. The bookcase against one wall held Andrew's farm books; Geordie had pored over them nightly, totally absorbed.

Pig Feeding and Management. Sheep Breeding and Management. The Dairy Herd. Animal Husbandry. Black's Veterinary Dictionary. He put Flash on the bed, and took the dictionary out of the shelf. It was depressing reading. He put it back, worrying about gangrene. The book had opened by itself at the word and Geordie wondered if Andrew had been reading it.

Suppose the pup had gangrene in that paw.

But if he had, he wouldn't be getting better. And he was getting better. There was no doubt about that. When Geordie sat beside the pup, Flash licked his hand and sighed deeply, beginning to appreciate his surroundings once more.

Geordie looked out of the window. Snow still covered the fields where the hollows lay, but had thawed from the rising ground which was improbably green. Over the wall he could see desolate moors stretching to the bulk of the mountains. Sunlight streamed across the farmyard and the cloud shadows were dark across the lower slopes.

Tom was busy in the yard.

Geordie wondered if the pup would eat. Perhaps just a little fish or some of the chicken they had for lunch; or would it make him sick? He went down to find Andrew, carrying Flash snuggled securely in his arms, and arrived in the big kitchen just as a large new car drew up in the farmyard.

Geordie loved the kitchen almost more than his bedroom. Already he was planning bringing his own pictures to put in the attic room. This would be his home for the rest of his life; the big room, the window seat where the cats curled in the sun, on the soft cushions where he would sit to do his homework; the scrubbed white table where Andrew sat at night with his record books. There were already entries about this year's lambs; six new lambs and the orphan whose mother had died and which would be Geordie's responsibility to bottle-feed, Tom had said, so long as it survived the first few days.

The kitchen was papered on three sides with a plain paper; on the fourth wall Shire horses cantered up and down, heavy black beauties, kicking up their hooves. Andrew's father had once bred Shires, but no one could afford them today, Andrew said, though with the price of fuel for the tractor and of petrol for the cars rising all the time, maybe they'd all be going back to horses yet.

The hearth was clean and swept; the fire burning brightly; the wooden highly polished overmantel reflected the flames, and Flash sat to watch his shadow, his ears pricked, the brightly interested expression back on his face. Geordie laughed as the pup moved his head and watched the black shadow ears turn too.

He glanced up at the calendar, on which two large Shires pulled a plough across an immense field. Twelve days since Grandy had been buried and he hadn't even been able to go to her funeral. Andrew had promised to take him to buy flowers to put on her grave. He did not want to go; Grandy and he had visited his parents' grave and the green mound and headstone had nothing to do with them at all. He wanted to remember them playing with him, laughing with him, not dead and buried in the ground and he wanted to remember Grandy as she had been in life; and he also had to face the fear that he had been the cause of her death; she was too old to look after a boy and he had never helped her much; never even thought of her being ill, or tired. Everyone who looked after him died, he thought suddenly and desolately, a terrifying thought that made him want to find Andrew and Tom and assure himself that both of them were alive and well, and not suddenly dropped dead in byre or stable.

Life was frighteningly unpredictable.

There had been voices outside, and now they came inside. A strange woman's voice; and a strange man. Geordie stood up, not wishing to be found cuddling his pup, and Flash, startled by strangers coming into the room, barked for the first time in his life, a high falsetto yelp that appeared to surprise him as much as it astounded Andrew and Geordie.

'He *is* better,' Andrew said. 'Geordie, this is your cousin Jennie from Manchester.'

'I've come to take you home with me,' Jennie said. Geordie stared at her. She was younger than Andrew, and pretty, with curly red hair and a pleasant face and smile. She was very tall, and the smartly dressed man who stood beside her, frowning slightly, was even taller than Andrew.

Geordie did not know what to say. It had never occurred to him that he would have to leave Andrew.

'This is my fiancé, Jonathan Broome,' Jennie said. 'He very kindly drove me up to fetch you, as I have to be back in school tomorrow. I'm a teacher. I've made my spare room all ready for you; you'll like it, Geordie.'

Geordie said nothing. He felt as if he were a parcel, to be wrapped up and taken away; never consulted as to what *he* wanted. He wanted to be back again, safe; with his parents alive and none of this happening. Except for Flash. If he had Flash, it wouldn't be so bad.

'Perhaps you could pack some things and send the rest later,' Jennie said to Andrew. 'I'm sure you don't want to be bothered with a boy about the place when you're so busy. We are very grateful to you for looking after him.'

'I can pack,' Geordie said. He marched out of the room, determined not to show Andrew that he cared. So Andrew didn't want him and had telephoned this beastly cousin, and he was to go off to Manchester; to live in a ghastly flat in a ghastly town; in England. He had never been further south than Carlisle and even that had felt foreign with the people talking strangely.

Andrew wished this cousin had not turned up out of the blue without warning; it hadn't given the boy a chance. And now, whatever he said, Geordie would resent; Andrew had seen the change in expression when Jennie spoke; the sudden stillness in the boy's face; the stony look in his eyes.

'I was quite willing to keep the boy,' he said awkwardly.

'He needs his family; and his mother and I were as close as sisters,' Jennie said. 'I should have been firmer with my aunt; she was far too old to have the boy. It probably killed her.'

Her clear voice carried to the stairway, where Geordie leaned his head against the wall and wished he had died in the crash too. He had not heard Andrew's words. Only Jennie, used to making her voice heard above classroom noises, had been audible.

Geordie climbed the stairs wearily as if every step were a mountain. His head ached and he felt sick. He wanted to cry but he was too old for tears and in any case would not let anyone else know how he felt.

There was a nudge at his ankle.

Flash had followed him.

He carried the pup up the stairs again, and pushed his clothes into the holdall. He had been intending to ask Andrew if he could collect the remainder of his possessions from his grandmother's home. There was plenty of room in the wardrobe and all the drawers were empty too.

He picked up the pup and the holdall and went downstairs.

'Will you stay for a meal?' Andrew asked.

'We must get back,' Jennie said. 'We'll stop on the motorway and give Geordie a treat.'

Tom, standing grimly in the doorway, knowing motorway food, considered it an odd sort of treat; maybe the female suspected they fed like pigs, whereas both he and Andrew could have got jobs as chefs any day of the week. He stared at Jennie, who thought him both uncouth and odd and dirty as he had been cleaning out the sties. She was thankful she had come to rescue the boy.

'Are you ready, Geordie?' she asked, impatient to get him home and make a start at knowing him.

Geordie nodded, and began to walk towards the car, holding Flash tightly.

Jennie caught her fiancé's eyes.

'Oh Geordie, no. We can't have a dog in the flat,' Jennie said. 'We're right in the middle of the town. In a lovely street, with trees lining the verges, close to the museums and art galleries. There's a wonderful library and a theatre; but nowhere for a dog. He'll be much better here and I'm sure Mr Grant will give him a very good home for you.'

Geordie stared at her, and then at the distance to the door. Suppose he ran past her, raced out fast and up the hills, and tracked over the pass to Angus and the twins. They'd have him, and the dog. But he knew even as the thought entered his head, that it was impossible. It was too far, and too much snow and Andrew and Tom would find him and send him to his cousin. They didn't want him; never had wanted him; had just made the best of a bad job, putting up with him all this while, and he hated them both for the false faces they had shown him.

He put the pup down on the hearth and walked out to the car. It was a Jaguar, a faster car than any he had ever been in, and he knew at once that he was going to be terrified, all the way down the motorway. It had been bad enough with Andrew; but the Land-Rover was built like an armoured car; this tin lizzie would crumple at a touch; and the roads would be icy and suppose they skidded . . .

'I hope you know what you're doing,' Jonathan said acidly, as they walked down the path. 'He's a surly little devil.'

'So would you be in his place,' Jennie snapped. She had not been thinking about the boy's point of view when she made her plans; but what other choice was there? And she had never dreamed of a dog. But he'd soon get over that; he would take a day or so to settle. Boys had short memories and the novelty of living a much more interesting life than he could possibly have had in the tiny village or the small town where his father had been a doctor, would soon compensate for the loss of the pet. He couldn't have had it long; it was very small; and remarkably sorry looking; a thin half-starved creature. A good job she was able to rescue the boy from a farm where an animal could look like that.

Andrew wanted to grab Geordie and snatch him out of the car. The boy sat there, staring ahead, and did not reply when Andrew spoke. The farmer watched the car drive out of the farmyard.

Tom was talking to Queenie again.

'I never knew such a bloody fool. Let the boy go without a word; off to some ghastly town, where he can't have his dog and will fret himself to death. Carried away like a piece of luggage or an old piece of furniture. All that one's after is his grandmother's money and the compensation from the motor accident. And the lad is no more to her than a piece of property.'

Andrew went indoors. The room had never been so empty. He called the pup to him, but Flash was deaf and blind. He had seen Geordie go and he sat in the middle of the hearthrug and howled until Andrew thought he would be unable to endure the noise any longer.

Not even Megan could soothe the pup.

Chapter Six

Terror rode with Geordie all the way to Manchester. Jonathan drove fast, overtaking ruthlessly, cutting in sharply, hooting impatiently at anyone in his way. They stayed in the outside lane, often exceeding the speed limit, twice touching a hundred miles an hour. Jonathan was proud of his driving, and was showing off to Jennie, who enjoyed speed, and had totally forgotten that the child's parents had died in a crash in which he also had been injured.

Geordie felt sick.

He wanted to howl like a dog, to cry for his parents and for Grandy and most of all to cry for Flash. He had never thought that anything could hurt so much. He could still see the pup's forlorn expression as his master walked away, could still hear the wail of distress that had followed them out of the farmyard. Suddenly he wished the speeding car would crash; would end in a tumbled wreck. And he would die with it, die like his parents and like Grandy. And never be hurt or frightened again. He had never felt so lonely before. Somehow, even Andrew and Tom had made him feel as if he belonged; he did not belong here, in this speeding car with a grim faced man he did not like and a cousin he did not know.

Please God. Please God. Please God, Geordie said, inside his head, but he didn't know what he was praying for. For his pup; for the car to turn and speed back to Andrew; for everything to be all right again, to be safe again, as it had been when the door shut at home at night, after the evening surgery, and his father took up a book and read to him until bedtime while his mother knitted and listened too, sometimes catching Geordie's eyes and smiling. The room had been a sanctuary after the day's affairs for all of them. Yet it was already fading in his memory. He could not remember the pattern of the curtains; only the warmth and the comfortable feeling of being home. Home.

He stared out of the window, and the old feeling of terror snatched at his throat. The world was spinning past. The sound of the tyres on the road, of Jonathan's impatient horn, of the engine snarl as they passed another vehicle, was more than Geordie could bear. He closed his eyes and leaned back, and presently mercifully fell asleep.

He woke in one of the service stations, as Jennie shook him.

'Come on and eat,' she said. She was feeling worried; the child looked green. He stared at her, completely dazed, and then began to shiver uncontrollably.

'I'm not hungry,' Geordie said.

'Come on and don't be stupid,' Jonathan said angrily. He had had enough of baby sitting; he had not planned on this sort of weekend at all. The boy was a damned nuisance and Jennie was an idiot to try and make a home for him. There were plenty of institutions to put him in and he'd be much happier with children his own age.

Geordie followed miserably into the restaurant. He had a lump in his throat so big that he felt he would never be able to swallow again. He could not talk; and Jennie, put off by nods and monosyllables, ate fast and determinedly, making bright chatty conversation to Jonathan, who was eating equally rapidly, in a determined silence that was as bad as Geordie's.

The meal ended at last. Geordie climbed back into the Jaguar, a small trapped animal. The endless journey continued. Jonathan drove even more impatiently. Once Jennie remonstrated as, unable to overtake, because of a car in the outside lane sticking persistently to the seventy mile an hour limit, Jonathan cut into the middle lane, speeded up and overtook on the inside.

Geordie flattened himself against the back of the seat, waiting for the impact. A sudden sharp braking frightened him even more, as they came to the end of the motorway and slowed for the main road. Here Jonathan resorted to overdrive, passing everything in his way. Geordie gave up. He was enduring, existing, the shivering so pronounced that Jennie was worried. The child must be ill. She did not think of delayed shock. She wished she had not been so ready to take on this responsibility. But she had taken it on and she was renowned for her obstinacy. No one would make her change her mind now and the more Jonathan chided her, the more determined she was to make a success of her quixotic idea. Geordie should have a home again; and a home with her. She owed that to her aunt, Geordie's grandmother, who had rescued Jennie when she herself was left an orphan at sixteen. She knew how the boy felt. And she would not hear of him going into any institution.

The journey ended at last. Jonathan dropped them at the door, refusing to come in. He was not fond of children and he had no time for this surly shivering little wreck.

He drove off as soon as he had put Geordie's holdall on the kerb, tyres screaming a protest as he ripped up the road surface, revving furiously. Jennie set her lips, picked up the holdall and led the way indoors, twisting the expensive sapphire and diamond ring round her engagement finger. Geordie followed, after one disgusted glance down the street. Nothing but houses; tree-lined pavements certainly, but tiny patches of ground in front of each tall three-storey building and only a yard at the back, overlooking another yard and the rear of an equally ugly house. The yards were separated by a narrow alley, strewn with broken glass. A black cat, one ear twisted against his head, prowled round Jennie's dustbin. The wall of the house next door, jutting out at right angles, provided the sole view from Geordie's bed.

He looked around the room. Jennie had left him, intending to heat some soup, as she was worried about the shivers that racked the boy. The road was still whipping past Geordie's eyes; the movement of the car seemed to dominate his own movements. The room was not steady. He sat on the bed, and reached out a hand automatically for Flash.

There was no dog there.

Pent-up sobs choked him, and when Jennie came in with the soup she did not know what to do. She thought he was crying for his grandmother. It never occurred to her that he was crying for Tom and for Andrew; for Queenie and for Mazabel; and for his dog. The brick walls outside his room, the airless atmosphere, the closed-in houses, had induced a feeling that Geordie did not recognise but that any adult would have known was claustrophobia. He had never before been in a large town; nor in any house that had not looked out on fields and hills. Here the streets were grim and grey and the view was flat and featureless; the trees were stunted travesties of the trees at home, and home was Scotland; home was the moors and the mountains; the lochs and the tarns and the grey-fleeced sheep running; home was a small dog, sitting beside a wood fire, trying to catch the shadows of his ears.

Jennie brought a cold flannel and washed Geordie's face. He did not look at her, ashamed that she should have found him crying. He sat in front of her electric fire, and drank the soup. It warmed him, and the shivering eased.

Jennie began to mark a pile of exercise books. She did not know what to say, and was shocked at herself. She had thought herself experienced with children, but she was beginning to realise a child in a classroom was one thing; a child in her home was something else again. She had had visions of a responsive little boy, eagerly accompanying her on all kinds of expeditions to the town's museums and art galleries, imbibing knowledge that she fed into him, helping her about the flat, chattering to her when they ate, grateful for her provision for him. She had not realised that Jonathan hated children; and she had not realised till now that Geordie himself might not fit her picture. She had seen him only once, as a delightful two-year-old. She had imagined him as an extension of her cousin; she had been very close to the boy's mother until her cousin married. It had been a pretty wedding; Jennie had planned just such a wedding for herself; had patterns for her wedding dress; had been exploring the possibilities of the various hotels for the reception, and she and Jonathan had found just the house they wanted. And, as she remembered that, she thought she had found a way to interest the boy.

'When I marry Jonathan,' she said, 'we're going to live in a lovely house on the edge of the country; a big black and white house. There's a lovely lawn where you can play football; and a swimming pool. You'll have your own room and we'll choose all the furniture together. That'll be fun, won't it?'

Her voice died away. The boy was staring at her, his dark eyes totally expressionless. There was not a flicker of interest in his face.

'Can I have Flash there?' he asked.

Jennie was exasperated. She was exhausted by the day; unhappy at Jonathan's reaction to her plan; he had railed at her all the way up and had frightened her too by his erratic driving on the way home. Geordie was completely unrewarding, and totally unresponsive.

'No,' Jennie said angrily. 'I hate dogs.'

There was a moment's silence.

Geordie stood up.

'I think I'll go to bed now. Thank you for the soup. Thank you for bringing me here.' His voice was formal and remote.

Jennie watched him go out of the room, a small, desperately lonely little figure. She sat, staring at the books she should have been marking, knowing she had failed the child, but not knowing how.

It was very late when she went to bed. She looked in at the boy. He was lying on his back, staring at the door, wide awake. He did not answer when she said goodnight.

She sighed deeply and shut the door.

The weeks that followed made little difference to their relationship. Geordie was formally polite, thanking her for meals, going off to his new school, where he sat in class and stared out of the window all day, pretending that out there, just out of sight, was a busy farmyard with milling cattle and the oily comforting smell of new lambs; that instead of sitting here, at a battered desk, trying to think about arithmetic and geography, he was back with Tom in the warm kitchen, bottle-feeding the orphan lamb. It would be grown now, its black face and smudgy knees giving way to its adult coat. He drew on exercise books; Derbyshire Gritstones and Rough Fell sheep; horned rams with shaggy fleeces; soft-eyed cows. He dared not draw a small black and white dog with a plumed tail.

Andrew wrote once, telling him that Flash was better, but very lame and that the twins had adopted the pup. He would have a good home at the vet's house. Geordie thought of the mountains climbing into the sky; of the loch below and the wind whipping sails of the little ships; of the rough hills where the bleating sheep wandered until the dogs herded them in. He had a vision of Megan, racing to gather the herd, her tireless little body running swiftly, crouching, leaping, snaking among the sheep, barking when necessary. He could have taught Flash that way; made him the best sheepdog on the hills, in spite of what Andrew said.

He was in trouble again for not listening.

His end of term report was atrocious, but when Jennie chided him, he only stared at her, under his lashes, and said nothing, an increasing habit that exasperated his cousin. Jonathan's visits were rare now. There was little talk of the new house or the wedding. When Jennie's fiancé did call he sat, smoking cigarette after cigarette, glowering at the boy, and Geordie, who knew perfectly well that he should have gone to his room, sat by the fire, and read, refusing to be tactful, while Jennie made frantic conversation and cups of coffee, and wished she had never offered Geordie a home. But she couldn't pack him off to an orphanage and there wasn't another person in the world who would have the boy.

The only bright spot in Geordie's life was the weekly letter from Davina, the vet's daughter, giving news of Flash. Once she sent a photograph, but that was too painful to look at and Geordie put it at the bottom of a drawer.

Life had a routine; getting up and going to school, where he felt even more alien than at Jennie's flat. His soft Scots burr made the other children laugh and he could not always understand their flat Northern vowels. They mocked him, and mocked his limp, some of the bigger and more bullying boys walking behind him, with exaggerated mimicry.

The only man he felt in any way at ease with was the biology master, Charles Vicars, whom the boys always called Chas. Chas had been born in the country and hated the town. He found out Geordie's background, having been worried by the small set face at the back of the classroom, and alerted by the drawings of sheep and cattle and horses that invariably decorated Geordie's rough notebooks.

'That horn's at the wrong angle,' Chas said one day, pausing by Geordie's desk. 'If it's a Rough Fell, and that's what it looks like, the horns are curved more. Did you live on a farm?'

'For a bit,' Geordie said, reluctant as always to reveal anything of himself to any adult. Grown-ups had a way of ferreting out secrets and he had no wish to have his bared to public view especially in class. Arthur Brown was already sniggering behind his hand to Willie Walker; there would be more ganging up at break.

Chas caught the anxious glance, and at break took Geordie off to help clean out the five rabbit hutches. There was one big black and white buck, a soft old creature that behaved like a dog, rubbing against a caressing hand, and Geordie, overcome with longing for Flash, held the rabbit against him, and tried to swallow the lump that seemed to grow in his throat at the least upset now.

He went back to the rabbits that evening after school, and helped Chas feed them, and then helped with the goldfish and the gerbils, relaxed for the first time since he had left Scotland. He found himself telling Chas about the farm; about the orphan lamb he had been going to rear, and then, about his dog.

Chas listened, recognising that here indeed was a child out of context; longing for the hills and the farm, imprisoned as surely as any animal in a cage. He watched the boy's face close again when he suggested it was high time that he went home, and wished he could wave a magic wand, and transport the boy to the hills where he belonged. There was nothing at all for him here.

Geordie did not want to go home.

He loitered, looking into shop windows, but wanting nothing from them. He stopped to stroke a Labrador dog lying at a gate and the dog leaped at him, delighted to be noticed. He knelt beside it, wishing desperately that it was Flash. When he was grown he would get Flash back. And then he realised that when he was grown, there would be no Flash, and anger surged in him, so that he wanted to scream at Jennie for taking him away from his dog.

He would ask if he could go back, back to live somewhere where he could have the dog; to live with Angus and the twins. Not here, where the days were always wet and grey and the endless clouds sat sadly on the smoky chimney pots.

He was going to tell Jennie he wanted to go back.

The decision gave him the energy to run, lagleg limping more than usual. He reached the house where they lived, and went through the hall, and up the stairs. Jennie's flat was on the first floor.

The voices sounded through the door as he came up to the landing.

'I am not tying myself to a woman who is always going to have a child at her heels.' Jonathan's voice was furious. 'I never see you alone. That damned boy sits there with a face as long as a yard measure, and he's going to haunt us for the rest of our lives. Get him into some Home; this is insane. Why on earth should you throw away your life for someone else's brat?'

'His mother was almost a sister to me, and his grand-mother took me in when my parents died,' Jennie said, equally furiously. 'I know how he feels. Poor little devil. He's not been here a term yet, give him a chance.'

'You have your choice now,' Jonathan said. 'Take it or leave it. You get him into an orphanage, or the wedding's off.'

'Take your damned ring,' Jennie shouted. 'I'm glad I found out what you're like before the wedding. You're a mass of selfishness. Never mind me, or the boy, or anyone else. Just Jonathan; the Great Big I Am; get out and don't ever come back.'

The door opened and Geordie hastily flattened himself among the coats. Jonathan stormed out, slamming the door behind him. A few seconds later came the sound of tyres protesting as the car skidded away, the engine roaring. Geordie stayed where he was. He had not known that Jennie had been orphaned too, or that his grand-mother had been her aunt and had given her a home. Family relationships were so difficult to work out when you were small. That explained a lot. Nobody had thought to explain anything to him. He knew Jennie was his mother's cousin but nothing more. He suddenly felt sorry that he had been so surly. She had been trying, but he hadn't helped.

And now her wedding was off, and all because of him. He brought misery to everyone who gave him a home.

He sat on the stairs, trying to control his thoughts. He felt very old and wearily wise, as if he had suddenly grown through three or four years in the last few minutes. He had not considered Jennie before; only himself. His new knowledge needed to be digested; her sponsoring him in spite of Jonathan; her desire to make sure he had a home, with his own family, rather than among strangers; her efforts to make his room a personal place, with his own belongings, and things he had chosen. He hadn't taken the least interest.

He looked through the tiny landing window, out at the red brick walls and the blank windows of the drab houses opposite. A sparrow landed on the sill and stared at him with brilliant blackcurrant eyes. Geordie looked at the draggled dusty bird and thought of the peregrine falcon, regal, and free, flying above the heatherclad moors; he thought of the bees, brumming among the flowers, seeking honey, and the sparkle of buttercups in the grass; he thought of the long sweep of the land to the foot of the mountains, and of the towering peaks where the sun flung cloud shadows in such variety that the shapes were never the same from one minute to another except on a clear bright day.

He needed to go back.

He walked to the window and looked out; at the tired street, and the pollarded trees that had neither grace nor beauty; at the minute patches of green, where a few flowers fought against the attentions of the cats that hungered for earth, and found only mud.

It was time to go in.

Jennie was in the kitchen, chopping onions, her eyes red.

'Hi,' she said, smiling at him, as if everything in her world were perfect except for the onion smell. 'Come and cry with me. We're going to have oodles and oodles of fried onions. They're a passion of mine, but the place smells of them for hours afterwards, so I don't often cook them. We're on our own tonight, and I don't mind the smell, do you?'

'I love fried onions,' Geordie said, with such enthusiasm that Jennie looked at him sharply, wondering why on earth fried onions should evoke the first genuine response that Geordie had given since he arrived.

Jennie cooked steak and game chips, and peas as well as the fried onions; opened a tin of peaches and another of cream, and Geordie laid the table, again for the first time. They ate in silence, but Jennie, in spite of her own misery, was aware of a change in the boy; an effort to be reasonable, so that he smiled at her once, uncertainly, but at least a smile instead of the glowering silence.

She was aware of her ringless finger; aware that tonight Jonathan would not hammer impatiently on the door; aware that there was a great gap in her life which would have to be filled; and, rather surprisingly, aware, as she ate, of a sense of relief, because she was free to choose what she would do; free to come and free to go, and would not be rushed off to a party or on a too fast drive along the motorways to a roadhouse, where the food was too rich, the music too loud, the dancing too frenetic, the laughter insincere, and the atmosphere airless and smoke-filled.

She would learn to walk in the hills again; the boy would like that.

'I forgot,' she said, as Geordie tidied up his books before going off to bed. 'There's a letter for you.'

She had not forgotten. She had left it, not wanting to spoil this new mood. Letters from Scotland always upset Geordie. Davina wrote about Flash and he ached for Flash, his first dog. There was never another dog like the first, though that was something Geordie could only learn through the years.

He took the letter, and then, feeling he should make some comment, and would have done had he not over-heard Jennie and Jonathan quarrelling, he asked the question that he had been hesitating over all evening.

'Jonathan?' Jennie's voice was light. 'Our wedding's off, Geordie. We're not right for one another. He won't be coming here again. Now, off to bed with you.'

She needed time alone. Time to absorb the hurt. Time to brood over the break in her life and the uncertain future.

Geordie could not think of an excuse to stay up. He went off to his room and opened Davina's letter. He knew, without telling, that Jennie did mind; he could feel her mood, and it affected him, so that he closed his bedroom door quietly.

Davina was an untidy writer, her letter full of blots and crossed out words, sprawling across the page.

Dear Geordie,

I don't know how to tell you. Flash ran away. He went three weeks ago but we hoped we'd find him. Dad thinks he's gone to look for you as he's been seen near Andrew's.

But he's killing sheep. The farmers are looking for him, and going to shoot him. There isn't anything we can do. He won't come if we call though we've been near him twice. He just runs off. I'm sorry Geordie. We did try. Dad said I had to tell you. I hope you like it in Manchester.

Love,

Davey.

Desolation settled over Geordie as he thought of his dog; alone on the moors, out in the dark night and the rain; so hungry that he was chasing the sheep and killing them to keep himself alive. A wild dog, no longer friendly to anyone. If they hadn't made Geordie go away . . .

He needed company and consolation. He went back into the sitting-room. Jennie did not see him. She sat in the big armchair by the fire, her eyes closed, tears, which she did nothing to check, running down her cheeks.

She had no consolation to offer.

Geordie went back and sat on his bed and stared at the lighted windows of the houses that backed on to theirs. A woman bathed a small boy in front of a fire; another woman held a baby against her, rocking it to soothe some childish upset; a man sat at a table by the window of a third house, his head bent over his work. Families; with children and parents together. A dog suddenly appeared at another window, its paws on the sill, its mouth open in an inaudible bark.

Only he belonged nowhere. He had ruined Jennie's life.

He read the letter again.

He knew what he had to do.

Chapter Seven

Flash could not understand that Geordie was not coming back. The dog drove Andrew and Tom mad, lying near the gate, leaping up every time he heard a car in the distance. When Angus came to look at the injured paw, the pup rushed towards him, and sniffed in the Land-Rover for news of Geordie, and then turned away, limping dejectedly back to his self imposed position at the gate. He would not come when called. He refused his food.

'He will be better with us; where he has no memory of Geordie,' Angus said, as he lifted the pup, and put him in the back of the Land-Rover. Flash curled up on a pile of sacks, nose to tail. He did not care where he went, if Geordie were not there.

Davina fussed the pup and nursed the pup; the fox hissed at him; Flash merely crept to a corner, out of the way and curled up again. He refused to eat again.

'That pup's going to die of a broken heart,' Catherine said, and went out of her way to coax Flash to eat, to follow her, to transfer his allegiance to her. He ignored her. He had no need of her. The other dogs shouldered him jealously out of the way.

Within a month of Geordie leaving the pup was feeding, after a fashion; he always ran to the door to investigate every car. Perhaps one day Geordie would come back. Neither Catherine nor Angus could bear to see the pup return from his inspection, tail down, ears down, heaving a long sigh. Geordie had deserted him; and he would never accept another master.

Spring was more than a rumour when the dog ran away. There were lambs on the hills, primroses in the woods, flowers on the slopes of the mountains. Trees were blossom-laden. The twins took the dogs out for a long romp beyond their garden, and took Flash with them, hoping he might liven and play with the other dogs. He was a very solemn pup.

Flash had never been outside the garden walls. He sniffed at the heather; he lifted his head and smelled the air. There were scents that reminded him of home; rank reek of sheep; the grassy breath of cattle; woodsmoke on the wind. He recognised that somewhere beyond the mountain was the place where he had been born, a familiar place, where he belonged. Here, among Angus's many dogs, he was an alien, not accepted, only tolerated because they knew well that they would be punished if they turned on him and thrust him out.

Flash ran a little way up the hill.

Davina called him, but he ignored her. His nose was working, was analysing the scents that were borne so strongly on the wind that blew across the mountains.

He ran. Home was there, and there too, might be Geordie.

Davina and Donald chased the dog, calling, but he only ran faster, and they could not catch up. His small body drove him over the heather, so that he was lost to them very soon, and they had to go home and confess that Flash had run off . . .

Angus was not pleased.

They hunted for the dog for two days, but there was no sign of him, anywhere.

Flash ran until he was exhausted, and then dropped to rest by a mountain burn that spilled out of the rocks. He drank briefly, and lay panting, savouring the sunshine that warmed him as it reflected from the stones round him. He watched a bird dip itself in the water, and preen; he watched a circling hawk, and then he slept.

When he woke, the sun had slipped behind the mountains, and it was cold and dark. There were stars in a remote sky, and the world was very large and suddenly, very frightening. An owl hooted, long and low, and was answered by its mate. There was the sharp tang of a running fox; the taint of a rat running near; the scent of rabbit.

Rabbit.

Flash had never hunted for food, had never been left hungry in his life, but now instincts that were buried roused in him. He needed no instruction. He had all the lore of his sheep-herding ancestors behind him, so that he knew how to run without frightening the small creature that browsed unheeding; knew how to crouch; knew how to make the final snaking run and the quick neck-biting kill. He fed on warm raw meat, for the first time in his life, and with the meal, the memory of civilisation deserted him. He was a wild dog, belonging nowhere. He had no master. He found a narrow cave in the rock and crept there, out of the wind, and slept, full fed.

Age-old instinct taught him. He learned to find shelter from the rain among the craggy tumbled rocks. He learned to herd the sheep, for fun, packing them on the hill. There were no farms near, and no one saw him for the whole of the first three days. His black and white coat was matted with rain and mud, but he was savouring freedom, and somewhere in his small head an instinct made him decide that if he could not be Geordie's dog, he would be his own master and live wild.

He was still a pup; half grown, half taught. On the second evening of his freedom he came upon four fox cubs. He was used to Angus's pet fox. He watched them play, pushing one another with small sharp-nosed heads, rolling together in mock battle, nibbling at ears and paws. The vixen was hunting and the cubs were alone in a grassy dell on the hollow of the hill, awaiting her return. They were as big as Flash, their infant coats giving way to the rusty adult fur.

One of them, a dog fox, saw the collie and came forward, curious. He stood, one paw raised, his nose sniffing. His mother had taught him not to trust strangers whether two legged or four legged, or flaunting down the wind from the sky above. They ran from shadows. They ran from cloud shapes on the ground; they ran from the stoat and the weasel. But they had never met dog, and he seemed like one of them.

The cub bent his front legs in invitation and Flash flirted his tail, and began to romp, his small black and white body vivid among the reddish fur. They played at tag; and rolled together, biting and kicking, until the vixen returned, a rabbit in her mouth. At her enquiring bark, as she came down the hillside, Flash vanished, knowing she would never allow him to remain, and remembering the still painful paw that caused him to limp on three legs when it began to ache. The poison had gone, but the muscles were drawn tight, shortened as the injury healed, and Flash would always be lame.

He had learned how to hide the lameness, and he could run as swiftly as any dog. Now he skirted the stream, making his way steadily back to Andrew's farm.

Flash's herding instinct was strong. Again that afternoon he herded the lambs, unable to resist the need that drove him. He knew how to work; he had the brilliant collie eye that could master a sheep, hypnotising the animal so that it could only obey. Flash stood, patient, staring at the ewe, his beautiful plumed tail waving gaily, until the animal turned and walked where it was driven and the collie collected another sheep and another until he had herded all the stragglers together. Then, he began to drive them, working by himself, running round them, dropping low, moving them gently, patiently, in a huddle that no ewe or lamb dared break, as if it did, Flash was there, moving faster than a sheep could think, driving the animal back again to join the flock.

The dog knew the pattern he needed; knew that one

out-lier marred the perfection, that so long as all were together he could work them at his will, and as he worked them instinct took over, and the need to be with the sheep dominated every other feeling.

By night he rested.

By night the moon showed the clear cold peaks, still snowclad; the long ranging rows of pines planted by the Forestry Commission, high above him now, and the heather moors where bog sometimes betrayed a wanderer, and several times trapped Flash, as he made his way slowly back to his birth place.

He knew nothing of the mountain. He watched from a hiding place one late afternoon as the golden eagle cruised the air above him. Flash had never known eagles, yet age-old fear taught him to hide. He had never seen so huge a bird. He watched it soaring idly, watched it sweep to the ground; heard the rabbit squeal from the heather and knew that this was an enemy to be avoided at all costs. The bird soared high to the nest on the cliffs where his hungry eaglet screamed impatiently for food.

Flash hid until the bird had gone. He was hungry. He had not fed since he caught the rabbit. He stopped to drink at the stream, and nibbled the heather, but that was not food for a dog.

He remembered men.

There would be food in the village.

He ran towards the houses, keeping in cover, distrustful of humans. Humans had taken Geordie from him. He came to the road and watched a car speed by, and chased it hopefully for a moment, but it vanished in the distance. The dog plodded on. He was very small and he was lonely again. The car had reminded him of his master.

He came to a cottage. The place was deserted, the owner at work. Flash skirted the dry wall and ran under the gate. There was food by the back door, a saucer for the old tomcat who had gone off hunting. Flash ate bread soaked in milk, and turned just in time to dodge the old warrior who leaped at him, spitting and hissing, seeing the dog take his food.

Flash barked and ran back on to the moors, where a sudden storm soaked his fur again and hail beat down, half blinding him, enormous pellets bruising his body so that he raced for shelter, and finding none, crouched defenceless in the heather.

The night was wet. Flash found some protection from the rain at the back of a shelter where two horses were standing, trying to keep dry. The horses ignored him, enduring patiently as wind hurtled through the primitive shed, and leaned against one another for warmth and company.

The wind was rising, reaching gale force, tearing branches from the trees, tossing broken heather twigs, flattening the grass, wailing with eerie persistence over the moors, through the telegraph wires, and through the shelter. Flash quivered with fright, glad of the horses' company even though they ignored him. He watched the clouds tear across the sky; watched the wind whip rag-tails away from the moon; watched the bright light gleam on the ground, and then saw the shadow of a horse's tail flicker beyond him. He sat, ears spread wide, back erect, body quivering with excitement for the first time since Geordie had gone. The shadows danced and twisted as the long tails swished impatiently and Flash was totally absorbed, pondering the curious darkness that was alive yet usually had no taste or smell. He bent to nose it and, surprised, smelled horse.

He crept further into the shelter where he discovered two scattered hay bales, put down for fodder. The hay was warm and he pushed himself into its depths, and slept, conscious all the time of wind noise and the uncomplaining bulk of his two companions.

Morning dawned bright and cool.

The horses pulled at the hay, and Flash crept out. Both mares were used to dogs, and were unafraid of him, until later, tempted to go and graze behind the shelter, they found Flash waiting for them. His herding instinct had taken over. He eyed them, daring them to move from the edge of the shed, daring them to set foot on the grass. Every time that one or the other made a tentative step, Flash was there in front of them, barking at them, warning them to go back, to stay in the comfort of their shelter, not to venture into the wild world outside.

He kept them prisoned the whole of the day, afraid to move least he leaped at them and bit. They were not freed until their owner came with more hay in the early evening and Flash, hearing human footsteps, vanished in deep heather and watched the woman walk slowly through the field and drop the bale of hay, and cut the twine and tease it out for the mares.

The mares, delighted to see her, nosed her and rubbed their heads against her arm, and searched her pockets for the apple pieces that they knew were there. She fed and stroked them, totally unaware of the dog hidden only a few yards away.

Flash was attracted by her soft soothing voice, but he had been free for long enough to be wary, and he did not go to her. When she went, he left the horses and followed the scents that had been calling him, ate small insects that scurried under the grass, and drank again, and found an old bone that the fox had forgotten and gnawed on that until he had stripped it of every meagre shred of meat.

The next day was a Saturday; a bright sunny day that tempted walkers on to the hills. Flash hid from them; hid from the shouts and calls and the heavy thump of boots. The warmth tempted two hardy Scouts to camp. They set up their tent under the lee of a sheer rock face that protected them from the wind and went off to shop, leaving food in polythene bags among their belongings. The wind told Flash of food; of meat, in particular.

He watched the Scouts leave. He watched their shapes dwindle and disappear round a corner, and then he went hunting inside the tent, pulling clothing out of a rucksack, pulling aside the polythene that wrapped bread and cakes and sandwiches; and a foil covered parcel containing a pound of stewing meat.

Flash fed until he was so full he could barely walk.

He left the tent and made his way to a small cave above the burn, where he curled and slept, warm and dry and without the cramping aches in his belly that had dominated him for the past few days. The Scouts, returning, found chaos, and thought they had been visited by a fox. They never guessed that the intruder was a small half-grown sheepdog. They grumbled as they retraced the long road to the village and replenished their stores from the village shop.

Flash remained hidden, sleeping off his feed, until late on the Sunday afternoon when he started off towards Andrew's farm again, travelling slowly over a long scree that ended in a grassy plain crowded with sheep. The dog could not resist them. He herded them expertly, unaware that he was watched by two climbers above the scree, fascinated by his expertise, who, later that evening spoke of the dog to a shepherd they met on his way home, carrying a lamb separated from his mother. The shepherd was worried to think of a collie loose on the hill. It might turn killer. But he knew Flash was missing, and that the dog was only half-grown and consoled himself with thinking that the stray must indeed be Flash and that Flash was harmless.

He in his turn spoke of the incident the next evening in the local bar.

'There's a sheepdog working alone on the hill,' the shepherd said.

'It will be the pup that Angus lost, without a doubt,' old Rory MacFarlane said, brushing away a rim of beer from his hang draggle moustache. 'But we will have to catch it, all the same. You never know when hunger might prompt a stray to kill instead of herding.'

'Aye. Remember the killer beyond Inveraray?' Donald McLeod, the shepherd from the biggest farm in the district said. Donald had been the man to shoot the beast that had savaged more than a dozen sheep before they stopped the carnage.

'Aye. That was a stray visitor's dog.' Rory drank deeply before he spoke again. 'Townspeople do not realise the damage their pets can do. Last year there were four thousand sheep died in one county alone; I think in Lanarkshire; from injuries from stray dogs. And that's a tidy piece of money when you work it out; only a few pounds here, and a few more there, but four thousand sheep; possibly the whole farm profits in the area for the year. Townspeople never understand the ways of beasts.'

'Nor the ways of the farmers,' Donald said. 'We had a party of young teachers over the place a few weeks ago and one of them, a female, thought that you had to kill the cows before you could milk them. What kind of a person is that to be trusting with teaching our children?'

Tom Fazackerley, who had been standing at the corner of the bar listening grimly to the conversation, blew the froth from his beer, and looked up.

'Not even a woman could be so daft,' he said.

'You can read it in the paper,' Donald said. 'The Gaffer was so astounded he wrote to the paper. There are people believing the strangest things and not even knowing that a bull calf is a disaster when you need heifers to build the herd.'

'Aye. It would be a good thing if we could choose the sex before the calf is born,' Rory said. 'There is talk of such things. Though I am not sure I would want to know if a bairn were a lad or a lassie beforehand; we might well get the balance of nature wrong, with men choosing only to have sons.'

'And a rare fight for women,' Donald said, grinning. Rory had seven daughters. The women in the village said he had gone on trying for a son until his wife threatened to leave home; seven lassies were enough to upset any man's budget, especially when they all had to be wed. Morag and Elspeth and Cathleen were already brides and mothers, and wee Aileen was to be married to Donald's own son in the autumn, and still three more sisters to go. Rory was sure he would have no money left for his old age at all, with so many weddings. They had danced for three days at each one, and were already thinking about the presents and the whisky for the next one. Rory and May put on a grand wedding.

Tom had forgotten about weddings and was worrying about the dog. He was angry with Andrew for letting it go; and was sure it was heading for the farm and the Lord only knew if it would arrive safely; or if it might turn killer on the way. Let it get a sniff at an afterbirth and develop a taste for sheep . . . that did not bear thinking about.

Flash was dominated by conflicting instincts. He was a pack animal, and he was lonely. He had given all his allegiance to Geordie and no one could substitute. He did not want just any man. He wanted his master. He was wary of other humans; Angus had been kind, but there were other dogs in the house, dogs moreover that had only accepted Flash on sufference; dogs that had never allowed him a place by the fire, or to be first at the food. He had had to wait his turn; had to know his place, and he had slept alone, instead of beside Geordie's bed. The twins were kind too, but the twins were not Geordie and he had no urge to go back.

He was dirty and weary and only half fed, but he plodded on, driven by the scent on the air; scent of Andrew's farm and Andrew's sheep and Andrew's pigs; a scent that brought memories of Geordie.

The way was very long, even for a sheepdog used to traversing the hills. Flash had not used the road; he was travelling over the mountain, climbing high, negotiating the sheep trails that wound to and fro, always using the easiest path, so that he covered far more ground than was necessary.

He trotted on, drawn by an inner compulsion that would not let him rest for more than a few hours. He could not always run direct. He learned that marsh was treacherous, and skirted the boggy ground; he came to a precipice of rock, and was forced to retrace his steps for several miles. He came, late at night, to a pine forest.

Here the scents were new; the smell of resin, masking other smells. The dank smell of wet ground with pine needles covering it thickly, the tang of the cones. He nosed one, hopefully, lest it be good to eat. He had not fed for almost a day and a half, and then only sparely. The cone was dry and seedless, stripped by a squirrel; it rolled, and Flash watched it, and then ran on.

The slip of a crescent moon gleamed between the trees. There were birds huddled for rest; a deer watched warily from a shelter behind a shrubby bush at the edge of the trees, but the wind favoured the deer and Flash did not scent it. He ran on.

Between the last of the trees and on to the rough moor there was a tang on the wind that made his mouth water. He began to hunt through the herbage, using his nose close to the ground, hot on a trail that grew stronger every moment. There was saliva leaking from his mouth and the driving need to eat was stronger than ever. He ran on, zig-zagging along the ground, discarding the scent of mouse that crossed the track; oblivious even to the scent of sheep nearby.

The old ewe smelled the dog and got stiffly to her feet, and limped off through the growing heather, victim of footrot that caused her foot to ache and made her kneel to eat. She belonged to a farm that rarely looked over the sheep and the shepherd was neglectful.

The wind was blowing towards Flash. There was never a hint of his coming and the black grouse was asleep, and heedless. It was unaware of the dog until Flash sprang.

The bird died fast and the dog fed, stripping off the feathers with his teeth, packing meat into his belly, growling and snarling softly to himself, total wild dog, all memory of human hands and warm home and dog food forgotten.

He slept that night curled in the lee of a rock that kept the wind from him and that reflected the sun next day, so that he basked in warmth, and was too full to continue his journey. The nights were becoming mild; the pull of freedom was growing too; and Flash had learned to shift for himself, to hunt for himself, and knew now that he could find birds and kill them whenever he chose. His nose would lead him to prey.

Each day brought new experiences to store in his memory.

Each day weakened the human tie, except that, when the dog rested, he was lonely and being alone was alien. He needed a pack, whether canine or human.

Flash had been running wild for almost two weeks when the shepherd from the farm beyond the long corrie strode over the hills with his own dog, a big-boned splendid worker named Fly. They worked the sheep together, Fly bringing in the new lambs for marking, and the old ewes for inspection. Sandy Ferguson freed one five-year-old from a tangle of thorny sticks that had buried into her fleece; separated two lambs that seemed sickly and that he could drive home for attention. His dog brought the ewes to them; and then Fly growled, deep and long and low.

Sandy followed the dog's gaze. Fly was stiff legged, his nsoe and eyes and ears all pointing in the same direction. There, a few hundred yards away, a black and white collie was crouched over a dead lamb, the throat torn from it, the body part eaten.

Sandy sent Fly to chase the intruder. The dog ran, zig zagging swiftly.

There was no time to give chase. Sandy had other work

to do and whistled his dog back, cursing. A killer loose on the hill was trouble indeed. He watched the small black and white shape vanish in the heather and went to look at the carcase. It was still warm. The dog had ripped at the flesh and done tremendous damage. There was no doubt that it had been killed very recently. Few people realised how wild a dog could be; even a pet dog, brought up very carefully, could wreak havoc. Fido, or Fluff, poodle or terrier, all had the power to kill and the urge to kill that could not be denied when the hunting instinct took over and no human was near to call the dog off.

That night, in the bar, Sandy told of the killing, and faces grew grim.

'We will have to hunt the dog and either trap it and send it away to a home where there are no sheep, or shoot it if we cannot catch it,' Old Rory said, his finger stroking his beaky nose, his thick grey hair on end, his blue eyes fierce. He loathed a collie turned killer more than any other dog; it was sheer treachery.

'Flash would not kill sheep,' Tom said obstinately from his corner. He had been listening, and was becoming angry. He had never forgiven Andrew for letting the boy go away to a town. Tom, more than anyone, knew what the dog had meant to the child; Tom knew that Geordie had farm blood in him, had a feeling for animals that was very rare, and would never be happy in any work that did not involve beasts. The boy, like the dog, had an instinct for farm creatures; knew how to approach them, always gently, thoughtfully, never carelessly; and Andrew had betrayed him. The boy could have had a home with them, been taught by them, and Andrew had no one to inherit the farm; neither sons nor brothers, and his only sister wed to a townsman, and not likely to want the place, though she had no children either.

'There is no other collie straying,' Sandy said. 'We would have heard. And none of us has a dog that wanders.'

'Maybe a stray come after a bitch,' Tom said obstinately. 'They will come from far enough and Donald's Kit has been in season this past two weeks.'

'If he'd come after Kit he'd not be after the sheep; he'd have only the one idea in his head,' Donald said. 'He'd be at my door and never leaving it till I chased him off.'

Tom had no more to say. It was true enough. Even police dogs forgot their work and went after a bitch in season, landing their handlers embarrassingly at a house without any criminal to find. He swallowed his drink without tasting it and went off to tell Andrew that Flash had gone bad and was hunting his neighbours' lambs.

There was no choice now for any of them. Every farmer on the hill would be carrying his gun; every farmer on the hill would be against the dog; and it was only a matter of time.

Andrew listened, his face set. He wished more than ever that he had fought to keep Geordie. He knew Davina wrote; he knew that Geordie answered, and Angus had said that his letters contained nothing but questions about Flash. Was the dog better? Was he eating? What did he look like? Had he grown? Was he still lame?

Now guilt needled; one mistake after another; he should never have given the dog to the boy; but how could you be wise at the time? It was easy to see the truth by hind-sight; not so easy to pick your way through a maze of probabilities. He had thought he was doing right. Thought he was doing a kindness, never dreaming that Sheena would die so soon.

Long after Tom had gone, Andrew sat by the fire suck-ing an empty pipe, unable to face his bed. Megan lay with her nose against her master's slippered foot, and dreamed she was herding sheep and whimpered in her sleep.

Outside, on the hills, Flash crouched over the half eaten lamb and ate.

Chapter Eight

Geordie lay awake, thinking of Davina's letter. He had visions of his dog running on the hills, alone, untended, perhaps with that lame paw cut again, limping his way towards Andrew's farm.

Geordie had deserted him and now his dog had gone wild.

A sheepkiller.

Geordie knew what that meant in farming country. There would be no second chance for Flash. And Flash would not come for the twins, or for Angus. He would not go to Tom or to Andrew. But he would come for Geordie. Geordie was quite sure of that, and visualised the reunion, somewhere on the hills, his dog racing to him, eyes alight, tail wagging frantically, small body wriggling ecstatically, totally overcome by excitement. Geordie knew just how the prick ears would lie flat against the small black and white head, the way the dog's body would creep towards him, the way Flash would sit, nose pointing upwards, while Geordie soothed the sides of his head, smoothed the soft ears, gentled the dog until he calmed. And then, with a flick of his fingers, the dog would be beside him, walking close at heel, looking up, eyes on his master, desperate to work. Flash would never kill again if Geordie were there to look after him.

The church clock struck one. Jennie would be asleep. Geordie could not rest. He switched on his light, and dressed himself, and then packed his small holdall. He did not know how he was going to travel, but travel he would. He opened his wallet, a present from Andrew before he left, together with five pounds that Angus had sent to him as a birthday present. There was also his pocket money for the term, as he spent very little. There was nothing he wanted to spend it on. He had bought a new lead for Flash, sure that Andrew would invite him for the summer holidays. He took it out of the drawer, and added it to his clothes.

He would need it, and he would need a check chain, but at first he could slip the end of the lead through the noose and fasten that round the dog's neck; he knew he would find Flash as soon as he began to search the hill.

He switched off the light and opened the door carefully. There was no light under Jennie's door. The flat was dark. He slipped out on to the landing, thankful that the door did not squeak or creak and that he could pull it shut very quietly. There was a soft snick as the catch slipped into place.

Geordie held his breath.

Nothing moved, inside the flat or out. The moon shone glancingly across the worn landing carpet and on the balustrade at the top of the stairs. Geordie crept down, close to the wall, knowing that the centre of three steps creaked. He unbolted the front door, opened it, and went outside. He pulled the door shut. The lock snapped to. He was on his own.

In front of him the empty street was a long desert, the tall houses dark, the only light small pools cast by the street lamps and the faint glitter of the moon on damp pavements. A pair of fighting cats yelled suddenly in the shrubbery and Geordie jumped.

He drew a deep breath as he realised the noise came from cats and not from inhuman demons lurking in the undergrowth. He had never been out alone in the night before; the shadows were frightening; there might be thugs lurking in the bushes, waiting to pounce and snatch his money from him. He had more than ten pounds, enough, he hoped, to get him to Scotland by train. He couldn't bear the thought of hitch-hiking, driving in cars or lorries, knowing that each braking would drench him in sweat.

He began to walk, and as he walked, he thought of Flash alone in the dark in the distant hills, and the thought gave him comfort. They were both alone. And they were both making for the same place. Somewhere they would meet.

There were no buses till six o'clock.

There was nowhere to go, and Geordie was afraid. He stared forlornly at the bus shelter which offered no protection from curious eyes. But the shelter was outside a house which had a high fence, and behind the fence were thick shrubs. He could hide till daylight and then walk on and pick up the bus at another stop, as soon as he knew people were about and he would not be too conspicuous.

The house bulked dark, a large building set back from the road. It was a children's home, but Geordie did not know that. He only knew that the garden offered temporary sanctuary. He settled himself under a bush with his holdall acting as cushion behind him, against the trunk of a tree. He could smell damp earth and dead leaves, and the musty smell of dying vegetation. He was very sleepy, and he hoped it would not rain.

He dozed, and woke to find the moon had vanished from the sky and there was a thin drizzle falling. He huddled miserably into his shelter, aware of rain dripping down his neck; of the thin patter of drops on the leaves; of the aching cramps in his legs.

He watched the world wake up. He had never watched before and was intrigued to find that the first milk float was out before the church clock struck five, that the first paper boy was on his rounds by six, that the postman was working before six thirty. He watched the man cycle up the long drive, deliver the post and cycle away again, and then Geordie crept out, looking carefully up and down the street lest anyone should see him emerge from the bushes.

There was no one about.

He walked briskly to the next bus stop, arriving at the same time as the bus, which would, he knew, take him to the local station where he could catch a train to Manchester, and from there an Inter City train to Glasgow. His station was on the Glasgow-Oban line, and he could walk from the station to Angus's house. The twins would help him. No use appealing to any grown-ups. They would simply send him back. And Flash would still die.

The bus was half empty, the conductress half asleep and she did not even spare a second glance for him as she gave him his ticket. He had packed his clothes in a bag that looked like a school bag. No one would think twice about him. He wore his school cap, but intended to take it off when he was on the train, lest someone identify the badge and wonder what he was doing so far away from his school. Here, the brown and cream stripes were well known. It was a very large school.

He was not yet twelve and was small for his age. The booking clerk at the station did not query the half price ticket. Geordie sat back in a half empty compartment and relaxed for the first time. He felt sleepy and soon realised he must not fall asleep. He watched the rows of terraced houses as the train rushed by, and looked at the tiny gardens, some beautifully kept, others overgrown and weedy. In one a child played with a dog and Geordie's hunger for Flash was suddenly unbearable.

By the time the train reached Manchester he was very hungry. He did not want to spend time looking for food; and he did not know which station the Glasgow train left from. He took a taxi, feeling small and defenceless, wishing he could confide in the driver, who did not seem to find his explanation that he didn't know the town, and that his aunt had told him to get a taxi to the station, in the least odd.

He paid the driver, and walked forlornly into the station hall. His ticket bought, he had nearly four pounds left over, and he had half an hour to spare. He bought coffee and a ham sandwich and sat eating, feeling sure that everyone was staring at him and knew he was running away. But he wasn't. He was running home, back to where he belonged. He had not left a message for Jennie. He should have done; he had intended to write her a note, but in the excitement of packing and leaving unseen had totally forgotten to do so. Would she alert the police?

Geordie stuffed his school cap into his bag and joined the crowd on the platform. There was a thin cover of cloud and haze in the distance.

The train was on time. Geordie sat at a table and wished he had brought a book to read. He watched Manchester slide away. Soon they were beyond streets, running across bleak moors, the stone houses cuddling into the rising ground, often backed by trees. The grey sky did not help to raise his spirits. He watched a horse canter across a field and then he slept.

The train stopped and he woke with a jump.

A woman was sitting opposite him. She was plump, grey-haired and wore spectacles which did not hide the fact that her blue eyes were kind. She looked like a grandmother; a safe, serene sort of person, Geordie thought. The impression was enforced by her brown coat and brown hat; by her big overfull handbag, and the parcel on the table in front of her.

'Better for your sleep, love?' she asked, with a little smile, as Geordie blinked at her. He felt uncomfortable, having been too long in his clothes. His skin prickled and his eyes ached. He was still tired.

'Yes, thank you,' he said.

'Not feeling sick, love?' the woman asked.

Geordie stared at her, astonished, and she laughed.

'The last time I went to see my married daughter there was a boy very like you opposite me and trains made him sick. I've made far too many sandwiches and if you don't feel sick you can help me eat them. Travelling makes me feel proper clemmed, and I feel a pig eating alone.'

Geordie had been long enough in Manchester to know that clemmed meant hungry and that starved meant cold. He, come to think of it, was proper clemmed too.

He had never tasted sandwiches like them. Fresh home baked bread and wonderful butter; delicious fillings that he failed to identify; new baked scones followed and tiny cups of jellied oranges; and coffee bought from the trolley that came round and that tasted very good. The woman bought chocolate and shared it with Geordie, talking all the time, telling him of her own grandson, Stephen, and how he liked animals and how they went every Saturday to the park, to look at the birds in the aviary; brilliant little finches, tiny parakeets, canaries and budgerigars. Then Stephen played in the adventure playground while his grandmother took the load off her feet and munched chocolates.

'Stephen's Dad says I ought to diet,' she said. 'And so I ought, but I'm too kind to myself for my own good. It's a bad habit. Going visiting your gran?'

Geordie shook his head.

'Friends,' he said, deciding to stick as near to the truth as he could. It was easier than making something up and remembering the lie. 'They're twins. They live in Scotland.'

'I'm only going as far as Carlisle,' the woman said. 'We'll be there any minute now. I'll leave you the rest of my sandwiches. I won't need them and you look like you could do with fattening up a bit. No more of you than a cock sparrow.'

Geordie was sorry when she went. She had helped to pass the time for him, but he was very glad of the food which would save his precious pence. He was not at all sure he had enough money to take him on to the village where the twins lived.

He watched the scenery change; the town gave way to moorland, very like the moors at home. In one field a sheepdog herded the sheep, a black and white collie. The ache for Flash returned.

It was raining when the train reached Glasgow. Geordie

wandered forlornly through the streets, with four hours to kill before his connection. He was very hungry, but all the places that sold food seemed too grand. Looking for a cheap place, he turned up a side street, and here found a small café named the Sitting Duck.

It was far from exotic; bare tables with huge salt and pepper pots; a plump waitress, her smile vivid and welcoming, wiping the plastic top with a dirty cloth; but the food was cheap and warming. Geordie chose the soup of the day which was a meat broth thick with vegetables, with potatoes and onions and herbs, that both filled him and comforted him. After that came chicken with chips and squishy peas, and ice cream with a caramel sauce, all of it costing only fifty pence. He did not know whether he ought to leave a tip or not, but his money was getting short and he decided not, and worried over it for the rest of the afternoon as he wandered round the shops, glad at times to go inside and look about him, keeping out of the rain. He seemed to be everlastingly hungry. Food filled in the time, and prevented him from worrying about his future.

The Oban train left at six o'clock. Geordie discovered he had enough money for his ticket and more than a pound to spare. He spent some of it on sandwiches from a shop round the corner from the station and on two bananas and an apple, and then added a meat pie in case he could not contact the twins, who would, he was sure, help him.

No use going to Andrew or Faceache, or Angus; they would only send him back. If only the ticket collector at the local stop was a stranger; if it was Hector McNeill, he too would recognise Geordie. The worry nagged him all through the journey. The compartment was half empty. Two men sat opposite one another, discussing sheep prices. Geordie listened to the soft burr, so different from the Manchester accent he had become almost used to. It was good to hear his own kind of talk again. He wanted to join in, to talk of Andrew's sheep but it would give him away. No one expected a schoolboy to know anything about sheep.

'There's a collie killing the sheep on the hill,' one of the men said suddenly. 'Ten ewes in the last two weeks have been killed, and the brute has been seen feeding on the carcases. But no one can get near. It is a sheepdog run wild, and we are hunting it on Wednesday. There will be twelve of us, and we should be able to corner it and bring it down. It cannot go on. That is a loss of over £100. And all from the one farm. People do not take care of their dogs.'

The train stopped at a halt and the two men got out, without a backward glance at the boy crouched in the corner. Geordie felt sick. He had two days to find Flash. Two days. What had made the dog take to sheep killing? Hunger? Faceache said that no true collie would turn killer, there had to be a rogue streak. Flash hadn't had a rogue streak. He had been gentle and affectionate and had herded sheep gently. He had herded the ducks in the yard; he had herded a racing pigeon that came to rest. He had herded the chickens. He would never kill.

It was no use running away from facts. Flash had killed. But perhaps if Geordie found him a home away from sheep . . . every alternative was unbearable. Geordie stared into the darkness so miserably that he saw nothing and almost missed his stop.

He did not know the ticket collector, who had only started work that week. Geordie surrendered his ticket thankfully and walked swiftly through the sheltering dark. Angus's house was at the far end of the village street. Geordie did not want to be seen by anyone. He climbed the wall into the fields, away behind the houses, and plodded through the tussocky grass, tripping and falling, wishing he had a torch, worried now lest the twins would not help him, knowing that Jennie would have contacted the police, not knowing where he had gone or why. She might call Jonathan too and they would be back together in spite of him.

He had been up too long and was very tired. Thoughts stumbled in his head and drifted away again. It was hard to put one foot in front of another. He tripped headlong, having plunged ankle-deep into a rabbit hole, knocking the breath out of himself as he hit the ground. He sat, leaning against the wall until the sick feeling had eased, and then ate the meat pie. He would have to wait for the moon to rise.

The moon was half full, and the going was easier once the sky was lit. Geordie could see the trees dark against the grey, he could see the bulk of Angus's house. There were no lights. It must be very late, later than he had thought.

He walked on, making his way along the grass verge beside the drive, round to the front of the house. Davina would be the best contact; Donald was excitable and raised his voice easily. Davina always had her wits about her.

She slept in the little room over the porch.

Geordie had been collecting pine cones as he walked along the drive. He threw them, expertly, at the window. Click. Click. Click. Davina opened the sash after some minutes and peered out.

'Davina. It's Geordie. I've come to find Flash.'

'Wait!' Davina's voice was urgent. What else would I do, Geordie wondered. He sat with his back against one of the big conifers and was so tired that he fell asleep.

He woke, sharply aware of danger. Davina and Donald were shaking him.

'Have you run away?' Davina asked.

Geordie nodded. He wanted a bed; soft and warm and comfortable; he yawned, and yawned again, stretching his jaws so wide Davina thought he would break the jaw-bone.

'You'd better come in,' Davina said. 'Only creep; Mum hears earwigs wander across the ceiling and wakes if a fly breathes.'

The moonlit hall was eerie. Light glinted on the spears and swords and the bottles on the hall table; on the antlered heads around the walls and on a fox mask that Geordie had not seen before.

'Careful or the dogs will bark,' Donald said and even as he spoke a crescendo of noise broke out. A door opened on the upstairs landing.

'Who's down there?' Angus called.

'It's only me,' Donald said. 'I came down for a drink.'

Geordie and Davina crouched behind the coats draping the armless Venus.

'For heaven's sake,' his father said. 'Hurry up and get back to bed.'

Donald turned and headed for the kitchen, making a noise, speaking to the dogs, while Davina took Geordie's hands and led him along the carpeted landing, up the second flight of stairs to the attics. She opened a door and they were inside a room in which was stored the junk of ages; more heads and brushes mounted on shields; piled trunks and boxes, and some battered furniture; a large dog basket and several cat cages.

'There's a camp bed in the far corner,' Davina whispered. 'Donald and I play up here sometimes. No one else ever comes. Don't make a sound. You can come down when Mum and Dad are busy, and wash. I'll bring you food when I can. The bed's behind that old wardrobe. It's quite comfortable. I come here when I've got the miseries. There are some books there too. You'll be OK.'

The door closed behind her and Geordie moved uncertainly, taking endless minutes over each step, lest he knock something down and startle Davina's parents. Moonlight flickered leafy shadows on the walls and Geordie remembered Flash, chasing the dancing shadows cast by his own ears.

He dropped on the bed and lay staring at the ceiling, aware of uneasy noises, of rustling trees, of an owl hooting.

He removed his outer clothes and pulled the blanket over him. There were no sheets and the blanket was rough and it tickled.

He was so exhausted that he fell asleep and slept till Davina crept in with food for him, just before she went off to school. He opened one sleepy eye to see her standing there.

'Quick. Everyone's downstairs. Come down and wash. I've brought you Donald's clothes. He's gone outside so everyone who sees you will think it's Donald.'

Geordie slipped like a thief behind Davina. He had never been so glad in his life to wash. The water freshened him. He borrowed the toothpaste to clean his teeth with one finger, the taste clean in a mouth that felt as if he had been eating stale soap.

'Hurry,' Davina whispered through the door.

They ran swiftly up the back stairs, and Geordie went to hide again behind the old wardrobe, sitting cross-legged on his bed, to eat bread and butter and two sausages, a slice of cheese, a banana and a chicken leg. There was also a rather squashed tomato and an egg that proved a problem – when Geordie shelled it it turned out to be bad and the smell stank the room out.

He managed to lever the window open a crack and hurl the egg into the garden, hoping the dogs would not find it and that if they did eat it, it wouldn't make them ill. It didn't seem very easy to keep successfully hidden; or very comfortable, and he had not had nearly enough to eat.

There were several books on the floor beside the camp bed.

Geordie chose one of them and settled down to read. He had never known that a day could be so long. He started at every sound, afraid that Catherine might come to the attic, perhaps for a cat cage or the dog basket or some other thing that might suddenly be remembered and come in useful.

His watch had stopped.

He tried to identify the time of day from the noises in the house. There was always a morning surgery and cars drawing up and parking indicated that animals were coming for treatment. Once a dog barked; a cat mewed, loud and long, a complaining Siamese wail. Then the cars drove away again and there was silence, broken twice by the ringing telephone that made Geordie jump.

Once he heard a pattering of claws in the corridor outside, and there was long snuffling at the door. The dogs would scent him. They would give him away.

Then Catherine's voice called upstairs.

'Mac, come down at once, you bad dog. What are you doing up there?'

It would never occur to anyone that he was hidden up here. Geordie breathed again.

He was so hungry by the time that Davina came that he could have snapped at her in fury for being so long. She had a holdall with her.

'I've been shopping,' she whispered. 'Luckily we've just had a birthday. There's crisps and biscuits and some ham and some bread and butter, and I've pinched one of the kitchen knives. There's some custard tarts; they'll keep. Donald's going to have a barbecue tonight and we'll boil you some eggs and do some sausages. There's cheese and some bananas. We told the post office we were having a picnic tomorrow.'

'They're going to look for Flash tomorrow,' Geordie said.

'We'll be out before them,' Davina promised. 'We're not going to school. It's a holiday as our headmaster's died. Not this one, but the one before, and everyone's going to the funeral. At least, all the teachers are. There's some chocolate,' she added, looking at it wistfully.

'I don't like that kind,' Geordie said untruthfully, knowing that Davina liked it very much.

'Oh, goodie, then I can be a pig without Donald to tell me I'll get fat,' Davina said and stretched herself out blissfully and began to munch.

'There's a flask of milk, too,' Davina said. 'I didn't dare make tea.'

Geordie was too hungry to talk. He sat eating, wondering just how they were going to find Flash in the morning. And what they were going to do when they had found him. It was all very well to run away, but where did he go next?

'The police are looking for you,' Davina said, wiping her mouth with the back of her hand. 'It's in the paper. Mum and Dad were talking about it. They think you'll make for Andrew's farm. They said you would never settle in a town. Was it awful?'

'Yes,' Geordie said. He didn't want to talk about it. Perhaps he ought to leave the house, now before he got the twins into trouble. He told Davina about the dog snuffling at the crack beneath the door.

'You'd better hide in the old shepherd's hut tonight,' Davina said. 'They don't use it any more. They take the sheep down near to the farm for lambing. We'll take you there later on. Mum and Dad are out this evening. We can leave while they're out; and you can have a bath and some food and a hot drink. They said we could have anyone we liked in to keep us company so long as we only had one extra and it was someone Mum and Dad know. We don't need to tell them it's you. Just it's a boy from school and he's used to animals. You have to be in *this* house.'

Geordie set his watch by Davina's; he had completely forgotten to wind it. He stretched out on the bed again when Davina left; he had food and drink and something to read, but for all that he was aware of loneliness and of the noises in the house; a door banging, an enraged barking from the dogs, a cat crying, as it awaited operation, a sudden snarl from a dog outside as it came for treatment, the coming and going of cars. He dared not look through the window, in case he was seen. He watched the branches shift in the wind and a pigeon stare through the window. There was a soft insistent noise from some unidentified bird in the tree.

He riffled through the pile of books and found a detective story. It proved to be fast-paced and well-written and for the first time since he had left Jennie, Geordie forgot all his problems. He was so immersed in the story that he jumped when the door opened.

'Come on down. They've gone,' Davina said.

It was good to walk downstairs without worrying about noise; good to soak in a hot bath and to dress in Donald's clean clothes. His own were unbelievably dirty. It was good to walk into the warm kitchen and be greeted by the cats and dogs, though not so good to remember that Flash had been here and lived here with Donald and Davina until three weeks ago. It was good to drink scalding hot soup and eat the crusty new bread with butter and honey, and the apple pie and cream that Davina found.

'Mum said we could eat what we liked; we said we'd have our own supper, and have the fun of making it,' Davina said.

Donald was scrambling eggs; the twins did not bother about the order of courses but tended to discuss what they would eat next while eating what was already available. By the time they had finished Geordie was sure he would not want to eat again for several days.

For all that Davina packed the holdall with more food; with sliced chicken and ham; with a huge slice of custard tart, and another of apple pie; with a flask of hot coffee; with scones and currant cake; with crusty bread rolls.

'Mum'll just think we've been piggier than usual,' Davina said, though Geordie was sure she would get into trouble; he seemed to have more than half the pantry in the bag.

Davina stayed at home as the twins had to answer the telephone. Angus always left an emergency number, in case some animal needed him while he was out. Donald and Geordie left the house by the back door, climbed the garden wall and set off up the hill. Geordie looked down on the village, the houses patched with light, and the loch where two boats rode at anchor, their mooring lights brilliant, reflected in the rippling water. There was a soft warm breeze against his face.

Tomorrow the farmers were taking their guns and hunting his dog.

Tomorrow, unless he found Flash first, the dog would die.

Tomorrow, he would have to give himself up; he couldn't run any more, and if the dog died Geordie didn't care what happened to him. He wanted to hunt the hill and whistle to his dog, but there might be people about; and there might be others waiting for the dog to show himself.

Geordie stared up at the mountains, black against the sky. There was so much country – and where was the dog? He could be anywhere, but if sheep were moving, then the dog would be there for certain. The telltale flocks would give Flash away.

Donald was busy with his own thoughts and was busy too finding the way. He did not want to talk; someone might hear them. There were often lovers on the hills, and the village girls and lads might tell tales. And many of them knew Geordie.

The going was rougher, with grass giving way to outcrop rock and boulder. The hut and the old sheepfold were high on the hill. A startled ewe scrambled to her feet, bleating to a near full-grown lamb and the pair of them ran, alerting other sheep.

Once Donald gripped Geordie's arm hard, and Geordie glanced sideways to see a stag standing, sideways on, head turned towards him. He had one half-grown antler, and a tiny knob where the other should have started to come. Geordie knew without telling that this was a lone stag, very old, waiting to die. The beast snorted, turned away and plodded on.

The shepherd's hut was half ruined, the roof open to the sky in several places. The mud floor was dusty. Donald had brought two sacks which he spread for Geordie, who was wearing two jerseys and an anorak and even so was cold. It was going to be a long night.

Geordie could not sleep. There were noises all around him; strange snorting noises that proved to be a sheep snoring; a sudden enraged cry from some small animal running past the hut; a stamp of a hoof from either a sheep or a deer. Somewhere inside the hut there were noises too. Geordie crouched against the wall, and when the moon rose he found himself staring into a pair of glinting eyes. The animal moved and came towards him and he realised it was only a sheep and moreover a sheep that must have been hand-reared and was used to people. It settled against him and he huddled against it, glad of the woolly fleece to keep him warm, though he soon began to itch all over from the attentions of the insects harboured in the thick coat.

Day dawned at last.

There was light in the sky.

Geordie went outside. There must be water near. He had been conscious, all night long, of the soft chatter of a burn on the hillside. He could hear it still, but when he reached the door he saw that the world had vanished. He was totally enclosed by mist. Sounds came to him, distorted and muted.

The thick cloud was moving slowly, swirling on the side of the hill. It cleared slightly, revealing the loch, and then thickened again. There was not a trace of wind. There was only a small area around him where boulders and dry sparse grass showed that he was not marooned in space.

He dared not move.

He glanced at his watch. Almost six in the morning. No one could hunt the dog in this. If only the mist lasted; it would mean one day longer for Flash.

Geordie settled himself in the doorway of the hut, and

ate and drank. His spirits had risen and he felt as if he too had been reprieved. No one could visit him, but that did not matter; perhaps the dog would scent him on the wind, if Flash were near, and come to him. Geordie dared not move; but the dog's nose could guide him.

The food was good, the hot coffee was warming, even though the mist was chill. Donald had put a plastic sheet in the holdall and Geordie wrapped it round himself, to keep out the cold. He shared a scone with the sheep and nibbled thoughtfully at an apple. It was very hard to plan. He had been drifting along, from one moment to the other, without enough thought. He needed to think; he needed to remember.

He settled himself against the wall, to try and remember Flash's puppyhood. They had walked on the hills; they had played in the fields; they had played near the farm, and they had visited Tom Fazackerley.

None of that helped.

Geordie stretched out on the ground again, and the sheep came back and nosed him and then settled beside him. She was an outcast from her own kind, resenting her life on the hill, preferring the yard where there were titbits to eat and people to pat her and stroke her and take notice of her.

Geordie slept.

The ewe nosed the holdall, and found food and ate until nothing was left. Full and comfortable, she too slept.

Geordie woke, hungry, at two in the afternoon. The mist hid everything. He was still isolated. He did not know the way down the mountain; but he did know that there were sudden dips and drops and crevasses, between him and Andrew.

There was nothing to do but eat again.

Geordie looked in the bag. Torn paper and crumbs told their own story, and he looked at the culprit. She nosed him happily, quite unaware of wrong. He should have zipped up the bag. It was his own fault. He drank some of the coffee, and found a remnant of cheese.

He was going to be very hungry and sometimes mists lasted for two or three days. He could not move, no one could reach him. Donald and Davina would worry; or perhaps not, as they would think he had enough food for several days.

He sat, watching the mist swirl away and return thicker than ever, a dense white chilling fog that hid everything beyond the small circle of a few yards. Once a hind loomed startlingly large, and bounded sideways. Several sheep settled themselves against the walls of the hut, cuddling down against the ground. A wary lamb backed away from the boy and bleated for its mother.

Far away, a dog barked and sheep bleated frantically. Was it Flash?

Suppose the mist was local and that there on the other side of the hill, men were hunting? Geordie was desolate.

His future was as bleak as the world outside the hut, and as empty. And far away on the other side of the mountain, in brilliant sunshine, he was sure they were hunting his dog.

Everything he loved, died.

His parents; his grandmother. His dog.

Nobody wanted him.

Loneliness engulfed Geordie.

He wanted Flash, wanted the dog at his side, wanted the comfort of his presence, wanted the warm tongue on his skin, the black and white body welcoming him.

The future had never seemed so bleak.

Geordie lay still. The mist could stay for ever and he would die of cold and hunger.

No one would care.

Chapter Nine

Flash had been alone for almost a month.

He was no longer a dog that was cared for and fed. Basic instincts had revived in him and taught him how to survive. He had learned that men were unpredictable. Some shouted at him. Some threw stones. One kicked him when he went into the yard to raid the dustbin, and came unexpectedly upon the householder, gardening. The collie had learned, by watching, that the soaring eagle was also a threat, carrying off hares and rabbits to its mountain eyrie.

He learned to hate weather. He sheltered from the high mountain snow in a tiny cave, huddled against the far wall, out of the wind. He licked the snow unable to find water. Water kept him alive, as his food was very inadequate. He had much to learn, and nothing but his own experience to guide him.

He learned to read the wind. The wind warned him of danger; told him of shepherds walking on the slopes; of sheep moving on the mountainside; of other men about, hiking or climbing. He learned to hide, using the heather as cover, running low against the ground, freezing until he was as still as the tumbled boulders that looked like scattered sheep, backs rounded and heads hidden, tucked in against the wind.

The wind brought news of food; sometimes brought with it the tang of cooking meat, so that the dog lay in the heather, soaking the ground in front of him with saliva, with wistful remembrance of meals made specially for him; and of a place in the world that now seemed forbidden to him.

There were other enemies too.

Late one afternoon he was foraging in a gully where trees masked the savage crack of the land. The wind was blowing away from him, so that he was unaware of a stalking fox beyond him intent, as he was, on a young leveret that was crouched on its form in the bracken. Flash had seen the twitch of its ears; the fox had news of it from its scent.

The leveret smelled the dog, but sat tight, relying on immobility to trick the hunter into believing his prey to be dead. Fox and dog leaped together, landing above the hare, hitting one another with such force that both were dazed. The hare leaped away and hid itself in the crevices between the roots of an ancient tree, safe from danger.

The fox recovered first and snarled.

Flash growled in return, a deep angry note. He bit, as the fox jumped. The fight was brief. The fox was little more than a cub, but both animals were badly mauled. Flash had more wounds to add to a torn ear and a lame leg; the ear damaged by an angry tomcat, the leg always weak from the dog's early injuries at Andrew's farm. Flash limped off in one direction, the fox in another, and both went to sleep hungry and sore.

Flash was hard and lean. His small body was all muscle. He was ranging further than any sheepdog in the course of its daily work. He wandered aimlessly in an immense circle, the centre of which was Andrew's farm. The dog had an ever present hope that one day, Geordie would return. The memory never faded. Flash had given his allegiance for all time and no other man would own him. Often he lay, nose on paws, watching the farm below, waiting for the sight of a small figure running to help the two men.

The days passed. Flash learned to raid farms where hens roamed free and laid their eggs under bushes. He never touched the birds, but he stole the eggs. Once he was fooled by guinea fowl eggs. The shells were so hard he could not break them, but one fell by accident on rock, and he soon realised that if he dropped them they cracked open and yielded their satisfying nourishment. He took eggs from the curlews' nests; he took duck eggs, carrying them in his mouth until he reached a place safe enough to hide him while he ate his stolen meal.

He hated rain. It took hours for his thick coat to dry.

The need to shelter from rain drove him to hunt the hillside more thoroughly. Here he found an abandoned fox earth and dived into it, out of the storm that sheeted down upon him. He widened the den at the end of the tunnel and lay there, dry, for the first time for days. The earth became his home. Here was sanctuary. Here he lay and listened to men striding the hills, guarding the sheep.

He knew that guns could kill. He had seen rabbits die. One day, having hunted fruitlessly on the mountainside, he went across the hill among the sheep. The shepherd, seeing a stray collie, was sure that this was the killer that had already been reported, and peppered Flash with shot. The dog was almost out of range, but the pellets stung, and the dog added yet another fear to those that had begun to master him.

He tried to catch fish, sitting for hours watching the shallows of the burn, but the trout were quicksilver fast, and he was too slow. They amused him, as shadows amused him, so that sometimes, when hunger was appeased, and he was lying at ease under trees, the flittering shadows teased him, and he bounded on them, playing a lonely game that helped him forget that he belonged nowhere.

He hated loneliness so much that sometimes he curled up beside an old ewe that had lost her lamb and was not afraid of the dog. Though Flash did not know it, she was one of Tom's bottle-fed bobbity lambs, and had spent most of her own young life curled up beside Flash's mother, Megan, who mothered most young things. The ewe grunted when she saw the collie coming, and he gained from her more comfort than he had had from any creature since Geordie went away. The twins had been kind, but they had rarely fussed or played with him, preferring their own dogs to the small intruder who had been as out of place in the vet's house as Geordie was in Jennie's upstairs flat, shut away from the real world that contained everything he knew.

Flash's need for companionship led him to make odd friends. High on the mountain lived a tabby cat gone wild, taken to hunting on her own, away from man. Sukie had never been a home-loving cat. Farm-bred, living out of doors, she had been given to a cottager who expected her to be an indoor cat, keeping down the mice. She hated indoors and wandered away, later giving birth to a litter sired by an adventurous tom who found his way up to her. She kept her kittens in a leafy nest at the bottom of a hollow tree.

Flash came upon the kittens when they were just beginning to tumble about outside. He played with them, and they played with the dog, and chased his tail. He was so engrossed in the game that he did not see the mother returning, and was caught. Sukie chased him off, enlarging herself to alarming size, spitting and swearing. Her sharp claws raked his rump. Next day, the kittens knew him to be an enemy and fluffed and hissed instead of playing, so that once more he was forced to wander alone, hungering as much for company as for food.

Some days after he had run away he became unusually restless. Memory was stirring and he had a feeling that Geordie was near. He hunted, head lifted, nosing the wind. He had not fed for two days. He had eaten moss. He had raided a dustbin and found a few scraps. He was aching with hunger. Age-old instincts possessed him. He turned and ran down the hillside towards the sheep.

Sheep!

They were there, all about him. Ewes and their lambs, their strong rank smell almost choking the dog. He began to herd, wary, cautious, watchful, only too aware of men.

His instincts drove him mercilessly. Hunger knifed through him. He needed food. He needed to herd. He watched, licking his lips. There was a small lamb, weaker than the rest, bleating forlornly, its mother nowhere near. He eyed it, and began to drive it expertly, away from the flock. He drove the lamb on. A shepherd on a higher shoulder of the hill saw the pair, and swore, as the dog edged the lamb relentlessly, never allowing it rest, governed by an overpowering instinct for survival that he could no longer control.

Jennie was frantic when she found Geordie gone. She stared, unbelieving, at the neat bed, searched his wardrobe and found his leisure clothes missing. His school clothes were folded neatly on the chair. His homework was still on the little table she had given him as a desk. She hunted for a note, but there was nothing. She sat miserably on the edge of his bed, conscious of failure.

She had thought the boy was settling down; had thought she was giving her cousin's child a better chance than he would have had in the remote country village where she felt that schooling was inadequate and it was unlikely he would receive any training other than farming. She had no idea of the many skills involved.

She had no idea where to start looking.

She had to teach at her own school. At break she rang Geordie's school to ask if he were there; perhaps he had only gone out for an early morning walk, and gone back and changed later. She could hardly report him missing after only an hour. She did not know that he had overheard her row with Jonathan or that he believed he was the direct cause of the cancellation of her wedding.

Geordie had not gone to school.

Jennie rang the police.

A constable called on her soon afterwards, his presence greatly intriguing the pupils at her school. He took down particulars. She did not know where Geordie could have gone. Boys were so unpredictable. Geordie had never talked to her about any of his real interests. She knew Davina wrote to him, but the boy had taken good care that Jennie never should know how much Flash meant to him. That was a private part of his life; a part that he would treasure for ever; and so was the thought that he would return home and be with his dog again. He had taken all Davina's letters with him. Jennie hunted through his room after school that day, but there was nothing personal there.

That evening Chas called on her. He also had been interviewed by a policeman, as he knew more about Geordie than any of the rest of the staff. All day a dull anger had been rising in him. He was concerned about the boy and ready to condemn the cousin who knew so little about the child that she did not even realise that his main interest lay with animals. Geordie had once betrayed himself and talked to Chas about his dog, and Chas, who had been an only child himself, relying entirely on his own dog for company and consolation, recognised the intensity of the boy's feelings, and knew the total rejection of town life that Geordie was experiencing. Chas hated towns as well, but he had to eat, and good teaching jobs were few and far between, and rarely in country schools.

He soon realised that Jennie did not know because Geordie had never talked to her. She was nothing like Chas had expected. He had thought she would be a hard woman, unable to understand a boy's needs, perhaps an elderly, rather sour spinster with more conscience than sense. He found that Jennie was none of these things. She was bewildered and vulnerable and overcome by a sense of defeat.

She appealed at once to Chas, who had a genius for comforting the unhappy, and a tendency to choose his friends from those less fortunate than himself, feeling he could give them something lacking in their own lives. He had never been aware of this. He only knew now that

Jennie needed help and he was prepared to give it, regardless of his own affairs.

The fault did not lie with her. It lay in the past. In the long ago accident that had killed Geordie's parents and thrust him, lonely and defenceless, into a world where he had to find comfort as best he could. His comfort had been among animals; undemanding, uncomplaining, giving unstintingly of their affection to anyone offering them care and attention. Geordie was a born countryman and would never settle in a town.

By the end of the evening Jennie felt better. She knew why she had been wrong, and knew too that it was due to something she could not have foreseen. She had failed through lack of knowledge, not through lack of care. Chas reassured her about that. He was a man to trust. A man that children and dogs and cats loved without question, knowing instinctively that he would give them comfort and courage and would boost morale. Jennie found it a relief to talk to him. She had needed to watch her tongue for so long; to balance Geordie against Jonathan; to weigh every word. Suddenly she was thankful it was over. Jealousy would have ruled her life.

'I never understood,' she said unhappily.

'Geordie didn't want you to understand,' Chas said. He had watched the boy; he knew the barriers he had created, barriers that only crumbled when faced with the animals in the school; especially with the black and white rabbit that had reminded him of his black and white dog.

'Why not phone the vet in Scotland?' Chas asked. 'Perhaps Geordie has gone back there. He often talked about the vet's twins.'

But Angus knew nothing and did not think of asking Donald or Davina.

Andrew and Tom knew nothing either. Geordie had not been anywhere near the farm. They were disturbed to hear that he was missing.

Jennie could only wait.

She had never known anything so dreadful as waiting for news; thinking, wondering, fearing. Chas called every evening, and on the Friday night, when thunder was rolling and lightning was flickering in the empty room, and Jennie was almost sick with worry, thinking of the boy out alone, Heaven knew where, in such appalling weather, the door bell rang. She ran to answer it, sure it was Chas, and longing for company to chase away the thoughts that bedevilled her.

'Look,' Chas said, as soon as she opened the door. 'It's the weekend; and I have Monday off. The school owes me a day. You said your Head would give you leave of absence. Would you like to come with me to Scotland? I'm pretty sure the boy will make for the farm and for his dog. I've nothing here to tie me. I know it's a long drive, and Giaconda, my old car, is a banger, but at least she goes, and it'll be better for you than sitting here, waiting for the phone to ring.'

Jennie couldn't pack fast enough. She needed very little and was ready within minutes, thankful to shut the door behind her, to leave the lonely flat that reminded her of Geordie, with his possessions scattered through every room. She rang the police station and told them she was making for Scotland. The sergeant approved, knowing the agonies of waiting without news.

Movement was relief.

Jennie found it hard not to contrast this journey with the last.

Chas drove fast, but considerately, careful of other drivers, and careful of his aged car. He had none of the rush and panache that characterised Jonathan's driving. There was a leak from one window and a howling gale round her feet, and rain lashed the windscreen, but Jennie did not care.

Chas talked as he drove, commenting on the country that they passed through, on a wealth of rhododendron blossom in a wood, on the brilliant suburban gardens, the flowers shining in spite of the heavy cloud. He made Jennie laugh as he told anecdotes about the boys; and told her of the day they had held a Pets' Service at school and the children had brought their animals to be blessed. One boy had brought a goat. Rameses spent the rest of the day in the Head's garden, which he not only stripped of flowers, but also of washing, which he ate, and he strewed the contents of the dustbin all over the path.

They stopped to eat in one of the motorway service stations. Jennie stood beside the car, waiting for Chas to lock it, and watched the rain drive down, and listened to the surly thunder rolls. She shivered.

'I can't bear to think of Geordie out there alone, somewhere in this,' she said. 'Chas. Suppose he's dead?'

It wasn't a thought that she had allowed herself before. Now she had to face it. She was too aware of the terrifying accidents that could happen to a child alone; aware of dangers from other men; from motor accidents; and from menaces too terrible to contemplate. She shivered again.

Chas put an arm round her shoulders and held her close.

Jennie relaxed, briefly aware that she need no longer be on her own. Then, as lightning flickered and thunder crashed, Chas grabbed her arm and they raced, heads down, for the shelter of the service station.

Chapter Ten

The morning was misty. A frustrated shepherd, stepping carefully on boggy ground at the far end of the glen where his sheep were sheltering, heard the panic bleat of frightened animals. Helpless, he listened, aware of bad trouble, of the frantic *baas* of the ewes, of the high pitched replies of the lambs. He visualised the havoc among his heavy fleeced Scottish Blackfaces, as there had already been several lambs killed from his flock. He swore to himself.

There was nothing whatever he could do.

If he walked towards them the dog would slip away, and in any event, he had come without a gun. He could never catch the dog, and he did not want to risk sending his own collie bitch in to sort the killer. She was early on in whelp.

He fumed all day. Fumed until a breeze at evening dispersed the mist and he discovered that the dog had indeed run crazy that day. Two ewes were dead, their throats torn out. Five lambs were so badly mauled that there was no chance of saving them. The other sheep huddled stupidly, terrified still, and in the distance on the shoulder of the hill, the shepherd saw the shape of a small black and white collie, trekking high away from the rocks, away from man's vengeance.

That night in the bar tempers were savage and the men plotted.

Next morning was fine and clear, a hint of haze over the heather. The men gathered at the farm at the bottom of the Long Glen, dogs at heel, guns in hand. They needed to flush out the culprit, and then intended to make sure he never killed again.

But the dog was more cunning than they, and although they worked the hill all day there was no sign of him. He had either changed his hunting ground, or gone to earth, full fed, and was fast asleep. None of the dogs scented him, or found his trail. The men returned to the farms, but they knew that their grazing acres were now a battle ground. Their enemy might strike again at any time, and no one was easy. Conversation was slow and sporadic that night in the bar, and was not enlivened by Tom's memories of another dog that had turned killer and harried the flocks for almost a year before it was killed in its turn.

'It's likely enough it's that pup you gave to Geordie,' the shepherd from the Long Glen said, as he had said many times before. He wiped froth from his moustache and glared at Tom, blaming him for all the damage.

'You mean our Flash,' Tom said. He was not prepared to admit that it was Flash that was killing sheep. There were dozens of dogs in the area. Some holidaymakers might well have lost a dog there, and, abandoned, it would revert to wild instincts again. Tom knew well enough that a dog running on its own might turn and eat the sheep it was supposed to guard, out of desperation. No sane animal would stay hungry when there was meat for the taking. All the same, Tom was reluctant to admit that the killer was indeed Flash.

'A dog turned killer has no right to a name,' the shepherd said angrily. He could visualise the mutilated bodies and the small shape trekking high. It had cost him a pretty penny. The dog was entitled to nothing now. Only to a quick death, and the quicker the better. 'He's not a dog any more. He's as wild as a fox and ten times more dangerous as he knows how to herd the sheep and single them. He's a rogue. A killer.'

Tom emptied his glass and said nothing. There was nothing that he could say. It was the end of all conversation. The men went out, one by one, into the night, barely speaking to one another, each one with his mind on his sheep on the hill, wondering what the morning would bring.

149

Tom strode home, wishing the clock back. No use wishing. You coped with what came and put up with it. He sighed and looked up at the moon. A new moon, glittering like newly polished brass. He turned his money in his pocket and wished, but he knew as he formulated the wish that it was futile.

High above Tom, unknown to him, the killer was working. He had rounded several sheep, and was now intent on singling out the weakling of the lambs, running swiftly, separating it from the rest of the flock. The dog worked intently, every instinct aiding it in its object. It had worked the same way before, and would again, and now knew how to kill. Tom heard the bleating of the terrified lamb, and raced up the hill, risking broken bones, or at very least, a turned ankle on the uneven ground, but he could not find the place, or trace the cries, and it was far too dark for hunting.

He called in at Andrew's farm on the way home.

'There's more lambs dead to find in the morning,' he said heavily, when Andrew came, tieless, in shirtsleeves, to answer the knock on the kitchen door. 'I heard the damn dog working the sheep again. Couldn't see a thing. It's as black on the mountain as the inside of Queenie's sty.'

Andrew said nothing. There was nothing to say. He shut the door again and Tom walked across the farmyard and paused at the sty door, but Queenie was shut in and sound asleep and it was no time for confidences. He stared up at the towering slopes as if he could see through the darkness, and will the dog to stop its deadly work.

Far away, mocking him, came the shrill scream of a dying lamb.

Tom slammed his fist against the wooden wall of the sty and swore as the pain brought tears to his eyes.

He hated killing a dog. But he knew there was no choice. There never had been any choice. All he had to do was to remember this dog was no longer Flash. The animal had forfeited all rights. Tomorrow they would be out after a killer. Much as Tom hated to admit it, the shepherd from Long Glen was right.

Up in the bothy on the far side of the mountain, Geordie waited for the twins who came scrambling towards him, after school, with a satchel loaded with food, having spent almost all their pocket money.

Geordie had drunk water from the burn and eaten two birds' eggs that he had found in a nest on the ground. The eggs tasted fishy, and were unpleasant raw.

'I'm starving,' he said, grinning at the twins, not wanting to say that he was so pleased to see them both he could have grabbed them and hugged them. It was lonely in the bothy, with only the wind noise and forlorn bird cries for company and the bleat of far-away sheep.

'You had stacks of food,' said Davina.

Geordie grinned and pointed at the old ewe that was standing, wary of strangers, in the doorway of the bothy.

'She had stacks of food,' he said. 'She ate it all while I was asleep.'

The twins laughed.

Geordie delved hungrily into the satchel, finding crusty fresh rolls, some filled with ham, others with cheese. Donald poured coffee from a flask and Davina took one of the rolls and munched thoughtfully, looking down at the loch, marvelling as she always did at the diminished size of her own home, the trees around it like cardboard trees on a toy farm, the chimney pluming smoke. The Land-Rover was a midget toy, waiting for a giant child to move it in play.

'They didn't catch Flash,' Davina said. 'He's too clever.'

It was no longer any use saying Flash wouldn't kill sheep. Flash had killed sheep. Donald had seen one of the lambs that had been brought to his father. It was the only lamb they were able to save. It had needed eighteen stitches in its gashes.

'He's gone quite wild, Geordie,' Davina said, her mouth full of food.

Geordie tore at his ham roll. He wanted to shout at the injustice of the world. If they hadn't made him go away from his dog, this would never have happened. It wasn't the dog's fault. It was Tom's and it was Andrew's. It was the fault of the lorry driver that killed his parents. It was the fault of the snowstorm that killed his grandmother. It was Jennie's fault for making him go away from here. Nothing was fair.

Davina watched Geordie, half guessing how he felt. Donald, who rarely knew how other people felt, and made many mistakes in consequence, twisted three long grasses into a plait and chewed it, thinking of nothing in particular.

Geordie was suddenly, savagely, unreasonably jealous of the twins who had everything; a mother and father of their own, a home, and dogs and cats. No one would push their dogs out into the cold or take them away. They had a place to belong to and he had nowhere. Jennie's flat was never home; she'd tried, but he'd hated everything. He hated the town; he hated the school; he ached to come back where he belonged.

He toyed for a moment with a dream that Angus would adopt him and add him to his own family. But that only happened in kids' stories, and this was for real. He was on his own, no one to think for him but himself, and no one but him to save his dog. And he had nothing else in the whole world. Only the dog.

He stared down at the ruffled water of the loch. He dared not speak. If he spoke, he would shout at the twins, would rage at them, would vent his misery on Davina, blaming her for his unhappiness, accusing her of carelessness and neglect in letting his dog run away. It was all her fault. If she'd made Flash feel wanted, had looked after him properly, had made him belong, he'd have run back to Tigh na Bhet, instead of running wild. But he'd wanted

Andrew's farm, and Geordie, and when he'd gone back to the farm Geordie wasn't there.

'I'm going to look for Flash,' Geordie said, totally obstinate.

'Shall we come too?' Davina asked.

Geordie shook his head.

'He might come to me if I'm alone,' he said. 'He won't come if anyone else is there.'

The twins watched Geordie transfer the food from the satchel to his own bag. He set off, his face grim, not looking back. He was going over the top of the mountain, and down towards Andrew's farm. It was a dangerous route, but if he followed the winding sheep paths he'd avoid the steepest places. He did not tell the twins. They might have protested. He knew he was deliberately choosing the most perilous route to Andrew's farm. But it was the shortest and he had very little time.

It wasn't easy climbing.

Sleeping in the cold and damp had made his leg ache. Geordie limped over the rough ground, pausing only once to look back at the twins. Davina waved.

There was a cool wind up here. And there were uncanny noises. It was easy to believe in ghosts and demons, to hear whispers from unseen people, to mistake the wind in the shrubby bushes for an animal shaking the branches, ready to pounce; to feel unease at the moaning whine across the ground; to jump at the *baa* of a sheep.

It was growing dark.

Darkness was a trap, as he was coming to an area where there were precipices. He would have to stop. He found a small dry cave, sheltered from the wind, and wrapped himself in the polythene sheet that Donald had provided. He was also wearing Donald's anorak which a mountaineer's jacket, well padded, and thick as a sleeping bag. He ate, and drank the bitter lemon that Davina had brought him and then curled up and slept.

He woke at dawn, stiff and cramped, his leg aching so

much that he felt slightly sick.

He had a long way to go. The winding trails, cut into the hillside by generations of sheep, were easiest to follow, but meant travelling much greater distances, as they took the simplest route, to and fro along the ledges. Geordie knew the sheep ways were safer. Where a sheep could go, he could follow. There was no danger from falling rocks or loose scree as the sheep never travelled over unsafe ground.

The wind was fresh.

Geordie stopped to drink from the burn when he reckoned it was lunchtime. He ate the hard-boiled eggs and the rolls he had saved from the day before. The bread was stale and hard to chew and he threw it to a bird that he did not recognise, and was briefly fascinated to discover the bird dunking the pieces in the burn to soften them before it ate.

Geordie plodded on, his leg aching so much that he almost forgot why he was climbing. The bare peak towered above, inimical. The sun had gone, hidden behind menacing clouds that threatened driving rain. The eagle soared, high above him, eyes alert for movement.

Geordie was so high that his chest and throat ached and it was far from easy to breathe. He felt as if he had been climbing for ever. The ground was rough and boulder strewn, and among the boulders were flints and pebbles that would turn an ankle if he went too fast. Yet there was no time to waste. The men would be watching all the time for a small black and white dog, chasing among the sheep.

'Flash. Fl–a–a–sh. Flashie boy, come.'

There was not a sound, nor a hint of movement.

The path wound towards the peak, and then rounded it. Geordie followed it, more slowly now, wishing he could stop the ache in his leg. It was a torment, growing worse as he used it. He needed to rest. But he dared not rest.

He limped on, reminded suddenly of the taunts at school.

Old Lagleg. Limping Johnnie. Lame Geordie.

And he remembered Willie Wylie, whom he had hated and who never left him alone, walking behind him, mimicking him, singing:

Oh where are the legs you used to have,
Geordie, my Geordie,

and who egged on the others to sing the words of 'When Johnnie came marching home,' with the name Geordie substituted for Johnnie. Drums and guns and drums and guns. The tune rang in his head. He hated it now nearly as much as he hated Willie Wylie. Willie had had another song, one he had made up on his own.

Geordie tried to thrust the unwelcome thoughts away, but he was so tired he had little control over them. The idiotic rhyme rang in his mind, and anger gave him the strength he needed to take him on. He would find his dog and he would never ever go back to Jennie, or the South, or to that school. He would stay here, somehow, even if it meant going into a boys' home in Scotland and making Andrew and Tom keep the dog.

Willie's words taunted him, sung by the wind.

Geordie's lame, lame, lame, lame.
Geordie's lame.
Limp along; limp along.
Let's GET him.

Willie's gang had followed him all through one hot dinner hour, mocking, irritating him, teasing mercilessly, and viciously until Chas had noticed and come out of the staff room like an avenger and sorted them properly, flaying them with his tongue, sending them indoors to do penance. Geordie knew he would miss Chas. And felt that he had let Chas down.

Life was too complicated.

Quite suddenly he was on the other side of the mountain, having rounded the peak. He looked down. There was Andrew's farm, seeming miles below him, totally dwarfed, and the village was there, dear and familiar, on the other side of the loch; there too were the garage and the hotel and the shop; the strung-out houses and the manse. He was home.

And he knew, as he began to slither down the steep slope, that home no longer existed. He had nowhere to belong. And what were Tom and Andrew going to say? And were the police looking for him? What had Jennie thought when she found him gone?

There wasn't a sign of Flash.

Geordie stopped and sat on a boulder, staring down, knowing that it had been a forlorn search. Flash was already dead. If he had not been, there would have been men with guns on the hill, there would have been men among the sheep, with their dogs. The mountain would have been populous.

Instead the sheep were at ease, scattered; fleecy grey shapes, blackfaced, turning to stare as he passed, or to move if he came too near. One ewe watched him, her half-grown lamb cuddled close against her, both lying under the shade of a large rock. He knew this hillside; knew every rock and shrubby bush and every grass patch; he knew that particular ewe. She had her home place around these few bare yards and though she wandered to graze, came back to it to sleep. Her lambs knew it as home. She often had twins, but this year there was only one single unusually large lamb.

Below him were other ewes, each in her own grazing patch, each having staked a long standing claim, passed on from mother to son or to daughter. The rams would be on the farm. It was not yet time to run them with the ewes. Old Mick, who loved bread and stole it when he could, as the baker often left it on newspaper on the porch floor; Sam, who was so arrogant he would charge a dog. Maybe they could put him with Flash and cure the pup of sheep worrying. And then there was the youngest ram, that Geordie had known well, a frisky beast named

Tinton, who had earned his name by an idiotic game with a tin can that Geordie had hung up to act as target for his air pistol. Tinton butted it and it clanged against the wall. Tom had christened him from the clanging noise. If only Geordie could go down to the farm now and find Tom and life could be as it was before, during the snow-up. But they would be angry with him for running away.

There too, was his grandmother's cottage, smoke coming from the garden where someone had made a bonfire. Somebody else owned it now.

The knowledge made him feel more alone than ever.

Geordie no longer wanted to go down, sure he would be met by anger. He should never have run away. Only now did the enormity of his action strike him. Jennie would be frantic, wondering where on earth he had gone to. He might have done anything; committed suicide even. Sometimes boys of his age did just that. He had read about them in the newspapers, not even taking it in. Only he didn't want to die. He wanted, passionately, to live. To live here, among the sheep, with his dog, to grow up and be a farmer like Andrew. He choked on the thought.

There was a ewe moving along the ridge. A second joined her and then a third. Something was shifting them. The sheep had been grazing, not a sign of panic. Now an anxious head twisted, and the shambling body began to run, the fleece shaking, the long pathetic nose turning towards something invisible to Geordie, hidden in the heather.

'Flash,' Geordie shouted, standing up and waving widly as he glimpsed a black and white back.

But the wind was searing along the hillside, bringing the sound of the frantic sheep to Geordie and carrying away his own voice. The dog took no notice. He was driving the sheep now, moving purposefully, working on his own, his body crouched against the ground as he eyed first one and then another. Then came the long low running and the instant crouch again, almost innocent. As if a shepherd were directing him. But Geordie knew that no man was there.

Flash had grown. Geordie had not realised how time had passed until now. The dog was far bigger than he had expected. Flash had been a half-grown pup when he went away. Geordie looked down on the dog, far below him, but near enough to pick out the black and white muzzle, the white chest, and the white beneath the tail. The ears, only half lifted before, were now pricked and alert, the red tongue flopped in amusement as the dog, his eyes fixed on the demented ewes, was enjoying every minute of his stalk.

Geordie began to run.

If only he could head the dog off.

But the sheep trail led nowhere. He had been following without noticing where he was going, all his attention concentrated on the scene below him.

The path petered out in a cliff face. There was no way down. Not without killing himself and nothing would be gained by that. Geordie sat reciting to himself all the words that Jennie had forbidden him to use at home, beating his fist against a rock, furious with himself for being so distracted that he did not realise that he was coming to a dead end. He could retrace his steps. He would have to retrace his steps, but it would take more than an hour to make the detour and that would bring him out far away from the dog and the sheep. In that time Flash could have killed fifty sheep.

Above them the eagle soared on a slipstream, knowing that there would soon be meat.

Below, there were more sheep, following blindly one after another and the dog was packing them neatly, watching his moment. If Geordie threw a rock . . .

But that might kill a sheep and would not necessarily panic the dog.

Geordie began to retrace his steps, half running, half walking, his breath sticking in his throat, his chest sore.

He packed food into his pockets as he went, and dropped the bag. He could return for it later and it hampered him. He did not know what he was going to do. This was not the pup he had left. This was a full-grown dog, self sufficient, his own master, having forgotten man. Flash was no longer a sensitive pup. He was a bold dog. A dog gone bad.

Chapter Eleven

Geordie could not bear the thought that Flash was indeed a wicked dog now, but he recognised that he must face it. There was nothing for it, he knew, but to let the men have their way. Flash would have to die. Geordie could never be happy, never let the dog out of his sight, as once he had killed, he would go on killing. As indeed he had. A one time killer would never again be safe.

He looked down, helpless. It was useless shouting. It was useless trying to run over such rough ground. He would only stumble and might break his leg again, and the memory of the long weeks in plaster in hospital after the road accident was much too vivid. And his leg hurt, a searing pain that warned him he should never have tried to scramble over the mountain, that he was not yet fit; that his life might be limited for ever. He might never be able to walk without a limp again, or to play games, or to climb.

The packed sheep were still bleating, their long notes borne on the wind. It was a fear-rousing noise; the deep *baas* of the ewes, the higher frightened bleating of the lambs, and then Geordie watched, horrified, as the dog singled out a lamb from the flock and worked it, until it was away from its fellows. The lamb was running dementedly, with the collie driving it, relentless, intent.

The lamb bounded over the trumped heather, dodging the boulders. The dog crouched and glared, and the lamb turned, trying to make its way back to the flock, but the dog snaked swiftly, crouched almost flat, and cut it off and headed it away, wanting it on more even ground where he could leap and kill.

Geordie picked up a stone and flung it, but it fell

noiselessly into dense heather. The dog did not even notice the fall. It was useless even to try. Geordie was aware of the eagle above him, aware of the din of the sheep. If only the *baa baa baa* were audible down in the village, but the wind was blowing in the wrong direction and was far too strong. If only a man were watching, a man with a gun who would end this, quickly, swiftly, for ever and give Geordie the chance to settle again and find his own way of living, a way that he now knew could never include this dog.

Oh Flash, he thought uselessly. Why? Why? Why?

He tried to reckon how far below him the animals were. Easily five hundred feet; and still a long steep way down. The scree seemed to go on for ever, narrow in parts; beyond him it was elongated; a long tongue of rubble, that would, Geordie knew, turn into an avalanche as soon as he set foot on it. Maybe if he went down with it the stones would kill him and his dog together. But they would kill the sheep too.

His thoughts milled endlessly, round and round, coming always hopelessly to the same impasse. Flash would have to be shot.

Geordie began to run along the path, hoping that in spite of everything he knew to be true he could call Flash to him, could tame him again and teach him again. Tom said that if you put a bad dog with a wild ram, then the ram would so torment the dog and toss it and scare it that the dog would never chase sheep again. Suppose they put Flash in with Sam. Sam hated dogs. He had once tossed Megan over a wall. She had run in and nipped the ram just above the hoof, furious at being treated so cavalierly by a sheep.

It was no use. His leg ached too much. The ground was uneven, and he had already turned his ankle once, and was hobbling still from the pain. He sat, unable to look away from the dog below him. The collie was crouching now, the lamb driven on to a flat area that was part grass and part rock. The dog moved so swiftly that Geordie lost sight of him for a moment, and then, turning to glance at the lamb, saw the dog leap, saw the wild tear at the throat, saw the gush of blood. The lamb dropped and the collie began to rip at the flesh. Behind him, the sheep, released from thrall, moved swiftly away, aware that danger had ended for the time being.

Geordie had to believe now. He had known when Davina told him that there was little hope; he had hoped that the dog was not Flash, but this was his dog. Of that he was now sure. He had seen for himself. He could not go down to the dog, not while he was tearing at the still warm carcase. Flash must be mad. There could be no other reason for his behaviour. A mad dog might bite even his own master. And it was some time since the dog had seen his master.

Above them the eagle soared in lazy spirals, waiting for manna. The killer had brought him an easy bonus; the dog could not eat all the lamb in one meal. Had the eagle not carried off the carcases to his eyrie there would have been fewer killings.

Men had been watching. Geordie saw them approaching, striding in a snaking relentless line, an army on the move, all the shepherds and farmers in the area, the game-keeper from the forest beyond the Long Glen, the three wardens from the National Trust, all of them carrying guns, a purposeful posse, hunting an outlaw. A sheepdog ran along the line. Geordie recognised Megan and saw Tom and Andrew walk purposefully into view.

A gun spoke, and on an instant the killer was gone, speeding into cover, taught by centuries-old instincts that never died, how to preserve himself. Nothing was left except the bloodied fleece on the ground and the head that lolled helplessly as Tom lifted the body.

Geordie crouched behind a rock. He did not want to be seen. He did not want to face men or face reality yet. He needed time to think. Time to come to terms with the knowledge that nothing could be done; that all his dreams were daydreams, the visions of a small boy, not of an adult.

Life was catching up too fast. He didn't want to grow up. Not yet.

He remembered the little hidden glen where he and Flash had once bathed in a pool below the waterfall. Perhaps the dog would go there to drink. Perhaps he would remember his puppy days, remember chasing shadows, remember sleeping on Geordie's bed. How did a pup grow up so bad? How did a child change into a criminal? What went wrong?

They were thoughts too difficult to face.

The glen was sanctuary; a long gully, tree clad, that cut into the mountain. Here the deer sheltered in the snow; here were red squirrels and once Geordie had seen a pine marten. Here too were wildcats. He had often heard them fighting, once had glimpsed a tabby kitten, basking in the sun, once had seen the quick shift of dapple pattern as an adult streaked for cover, far too shy to face man.

The sun was hot. Geordie wanted to rest; to ease his aching leg; to wash his gritty body. He hadn't washed for days. His eyes felt as if they would drop out of his head. His hair was dusty. His hands were filthy.

The pool welcomed him, the water deep and clear and cold. There were ledges where he could stand. The hot sun baked off the rocks, warming him. He stripped and dived into the water, striking out under the fall. It was good to swim. Good to relax; to forget why he was there; to pretend that he had come up on the mountain for the day, and that below him Andrew waited for him, and he would be going home to feed a bobbity lamb that had lost its mother; that he would be taking food to Tinton, and would then watch the little ram play with the tin can, and then, when Tinton was safely in the barn, would take his air pistol and target shoot while Faceache helped him and corrected his aim.

Geordie climbed out and dropped on the grass and stretched in the sun, feeling the heat warm him, clean for the first time for days. He dunked his clothes in the pool and spread them out to dry. He was a boy again, a boy in Alexander's time, far removed from today, one of the boys trained for the army, later to conquer the world. He closed his eyes. He was a messenger of the gods, running from enemies who would hound him down and kill him. He had found sanctuary briefly on high Olympus, by a pool blessed by Pan. He needed all the cunning in the world to stay alive; to stay unseen; to feed himself. He shivered and sat up.

He had cut himself off from his food supply and he was starving. The twins didn't know where he was now. He purposely hadn't told them. They would probably think he had gone to Andrew, if he didn't return to the bothy; and return to the bothy was out of the question. His place was with Flash, whether he was a bad dog or not, and Geordie knew that when Flash died, he must be there, to cradle the dog's head, and hope that in those last moments the dog would remember him and know his master had not left him alone for ever.

Geordie dressed, and ate some of the chocolate and the raisins.

The men had gone, having scoured the hillside. If they had come up to the glen, they would have flushed Geordie out. Megan was there, and she would have known him at once, and have found him, even if he were hiding. Luckily the wind was wrong and there was never a hint of his presence.

Geordie was exhausted.

He stretched out and slept, and the sun slipped lower in the sky.

He woke, startled by the touch of a soft warm tongue. He stared, not daring to move.

Flash was sitting, watching him, only a handbreadth

away, his tail wagging uncertainly. He was beautiful, even with his matted coat and muddy sides.

Geordie held out his hand, fist clenched.

'Flash, good boy. Here then, Flashie,' he whispered.

The dog inched forward, almost flat on his belly, his long tail wagging uncertainly. The warm tongue licked Geordie's hand again.

Somewhere below, a voice shouted.

Flash turned and ran, racing up the hillside, and vanished as if he had never been.

Geordie rolled over.

It was the end of his world.

Below him, on the mountain, Tom and Andrew walked back together, guns tucked beneath their arms. Megan followed them, aware that this was no time for frivolity. There were serious matters afoot and though she did not understand them, she did understand the men's mood. They were often solemn, there being little to laugh about on the farm, but today both men were extremely grim.

Megan was afraid that somehow, she had transgressed, and the anger was with her, and she was taking great care not to give further offence if she could possibly avoid it.

She watched both men, anxious not to miss a vital signal and earn their blame. Once Andrew, talking angrily, waved a hand expressively and Megan, thinking he had given her the signal to go left, flew out in a long arc, scenting the air, bewildered at finding nothing.

'That bitch is pixylated,' Tom said, using his word for pixy-led.

Andrew looked at her, mystified, and then remembered.

'I sent her out by mistake when I moved my hand,' he said, and whistled Megan in. She came thankfully, sure she had missed something she should have found, and approached Tom uncertainly, half crouched, tail wagging half-heartedly, expecting a reprimand.

Andrew was too good a man with dogs to do any such

thing. His own signal had misled her. It was only too easy to do. Train a dog, give a word of command and accompany it accidentally by taking out a handkerchief to blow your nose, or by scratching your chin, or lifting your head as something beyond the dog catches your eye, and in no time at all the dog thinks the signal is the command and for ever obeys something the owner hasn't even recognised as a signal.

'Good lass,' Andrew said, patting the bitch.

It was praise enough. Megan fell in behind the men, knowing she was not on duty, but that also she was not to run free.

Andrew's thoughts were busy with Jennie's phone call. He had been shocked to find that Geordie had run away.

'Do you reckon the lad will make for here?' Andrew asked. He wanted Tom to reassure him, to remind him that they had had no choice, but Tom had his own opinions about that.

'It's his home,' Tom said, ending discussion, not wanting to think of the lad on his own, so miserable that he had run away from his fancy townbred cousin, who would never understand the boy in a year of Sundays. They should never have let him go, but no use saying so to Andrew. The man was tormenting himself as it was, and had more bad news that morning too, as his sister's husband had died very suddenly of a heart attack the day before, and she with no children and no relative other than Andrew.

They could not go to the funeral as she lived in Cornwall, but as soon as that was over she was coming here for a while, maybe to stay, and Tom was not sure he wanted a woman in the place again, not even a woman he had known as a girl. Kitty had been away for long enough, living in softer country, maybe. Tom did not know the harsh North Cornish coast. She had learned different ways and had maybe grown into a tartar who would insist on better manners and cleaner habits, and tidier behaviour than either he or Andrew had time for. They got on very well as they were, and no need for the niceties and bread boards and milk jugs instead of the scoop they used to take it from the churn.

Tom did not like changes in his life.

He did not intend to reassure Andrew either. He was upset at the thought of the dog going wild and of the lamb they had buried, so robbing the eagle of his prey and robbing the dog of his evening meal. Had they been thinking straight they would have left the carcase and gone back to lie in wait, and shot the brute as he came to eat again. This was no longer their Flash. This must be a collie with brain damage; or maybe he had always had the makings of a wicked one, the evil in him waiting to come out. You never knew with any litter, just what would come, any more than you knew what the baby you had made would grow into. Every pup and every babe was a charmer. It was only later that you maybe had a rogue.

They turned in at the farm gate, still not speaking. Tom took the hose and the yard broom and began to clean the yard, working with savage determination, wishing they were back to the time of the snowfall, and Geordie was beside him, easing life with his chatter. He had been a happy lad once he forgot his troubles, and they were troubles big enough for any adult, let alone a wee one like that. Life was not fair, Tom said to Queenie as she rolled towards him, her massive body quivering with pleasure while he scratched her back.

'He should never have sent the lad away. It was bad enough, all the things that happened to him, without that too. He could have stayed here; or gone to Angus, or maybe been better off in a boys' home in the area where he could come and visit us and then maybe the dog would not have run off. I am going to shoot that dog, Queenie my love. It was my fault the lad had it. And I am going to hate myself and the dog for ever. And Him. He should not have given the boy a dog. He opened the gate of paradise for him and then slammed it tight shut. How could we live without you, my beauty, eh? Tell me that then?'

Queenie grunted, delighted, small ecstatic grunts, as Tom scratched and talked. What he said did not matter. All that mattered was the deep, kind voice, soothing away unease. Queenie did not trust people and she hated boys except for Geordie as some had once come into the yard and thrown stones at her.

They had gone out smarting round the ears from Tom's buffets and he had threatened to go and see each lad's dad separately and tell them what they had been up to and to get the price of the pig from each, pretending they had killed her. They went, totally demoralised. They were reasonable enough lads on their own, but together they lost all sense and ganged up and egged one another on, showing off, daring as to who would be boldest, cleverest, wickedest. Tom later caught one of them smoking a cigarette one day, too close to the haystack for anybody's comfort and determined to teach him the lesson of his life. He took him inside and offered him a strong cigar that had been given to Andrew some years before and told the lad to smoke it like a man, and not be caught like a small boy having a surreptitious drag.

The sinner gave up the stale tobacco together with his breakfast half an hour later. He would never smoke again. Tom had grinned to himself as he watched the small figure with the grey-green face stagger home, sheepish.

There were times when action was better than speech.

But this was not one of them.

Tom looked up the hillside, screwing up his eyes. So long as the sheep were quiet, looking more like boulders tumbled by a giant, than animals, then all was well. The wind was strengthening and would soon howl over the village, scream round the houses, tear through the heather, and not a bleat would be audible. Tonight would be a wicked night to be out on the mountain. The clouds were riding high, building up from the peaks, the great smoking anvil shapes presaging thunder roll and lightning flash and water swirling over the falls to flood downwards over the higher pastures.

Tom called to Andrew. Together they looked at the sky.

Andrew whistled Megan and walked up the hill. They spent the next few hours working the sheep towards the safer fields lower down. Tom hated the storms for then the boulders in the river bed packed and rumbled and when the water was in spate, flew through the air with the sound of a million roaring demons, so that no one could hear himself speak in the village, and water poured everywhere. With it came dead sheep and lambs. Sometimes the lambs were trapped on islands in the river, usually safe sandy spits where a small animal could wade and drink in safety, but which became death spots when the swirling peaty-brown flood hit them, the rushing torrent so fast that nothing could stand against it.

Tom suddenly remembered the story of the shepherd from the Long Glen, who some years before had sheltered one night among the trees and been drowned when the water poured over the falls. His ghost was supposed to haunt the mountains but that was one story Tom had never told Geordie, not wanting to frighten the lad, not quite believing, but knowing only too well that the glen could be disaster should anyone shelter there when the wind was high and clouds towered above the mountains.

The lowering storm brooded all evening. Geordie, hunting for Flash on the hill above the Long Glen, where he had last seen the dog, was unaware of danger. He knew there would be rain. Possibly tropical rain, but he had completely forgotten that the streams would grow within minutes to monstrous gushing torrents, sweeping everything near them away.

He caught sight of the dog working sheep high on the

skyline and made towards it. No use calling, as with the wind raging down the mountains, flattening the heather, his voice would be unheard. Flash had remembered him. There might be a chance yet and hope never died, not while the dog was still alive. Once Geordie stopped, unnerved, as thunder rumbled, echoing around him terrifyingly, an enraged giant beating on a vast drum, the peal reverberating eerily among the rocks. Lightning cut the sky in two, zigging between the clouds, blinding.

The sheep knew about wind and knew the thunder rumbles. They made for shelter, working their way to overhangs of rock or the thick clusters of bushes. The deer were uneasy too. A running stag thrust himself past Geordie, unaware of the boy, only aware of the demons haunting the hill and the need to get out of the way of the roaring streams, before the storm burst and put an end to flight.

The birds were silent.

The dog sprang and killed. Geordie sat, looking on. The animal was far above him now, running freely from one part of the hill to another, killing wherever he chose, killing, not for food, but for the joy of satisfying a new found blood lust. It was impossible to catch him. Geordie thought of the draggled animal that had come to him briefly and licked his hand. There was very little time left for his collie. The men were hunting. They would go on hunting, as long as the dog killed. Tomorrow . . . the day after . . .

The rain began, slicing through the sky, battering him with hailstones. There was nowhere else to hide. Geordie dropped flat in the heather, shielding his face as best he could. He was aware of the constant lurid flashing in the sky, and of the need to find somewhere, anywhere, out of the rain.

The hail ceased.

Geordie ran, ducking and dodging, avoiding the slippery patches of rock, knowing that a fall might mean disaster, or worse, it would mean death. Nobody knew where he was. It would be too late when they did find him. He would be dead of exposure. All Tom's warnings came back to him, and he knew the primitive terror of man alone against the wind and the rain, without a single person to offer him shelter.

There was a deserted cottage a few hundred yards away. Most of the roof had gone but the walls were still standing, and there was a little protection from the rain. He had matches and could make a fire. He raced across the open ground, his lame leg dragging at him, preventing him from the turn of speed he needed, so that he was caught again in a fresh downpour, and soaked within seconds.

He reached the cottage at last, climbing over fallen bricks and tiles, and settled himself under the shelter of a heavy door, put roofwise across the piled bricks by some other stormbound traveller. Rain drummed above him. He remembered that Flash had hated thunder.

Geordie crouched, shivering, wishing he had never embarked on such a mad adventure. He needed to be found. He wanted to be warm. He was hungry. He longed for a hot bath and a hot meal and a hot drink. He wanted to belong, somewhere, anywhere, perhaps even back with Jennie. He should never have run away.

Thought mocked him.

It was too cold for thought. Too cold . . .

His teeth were chattering.

The matches were wet, and so was the wood.

Men died on the mountains. They had died on the towering rocks above him, slipping to eternity; they had died on the rocky crags, falling, and breaking heads or legs or backs. They had died of exhaustion. They had died of exposure. And he too would die, alone, with no one knowing where to look for him. He huddled in a corner, trying to sleep. He was too cold. He stretched and yawned, and walked outside. The rain had stopped.

Below him was Andrew's farm, far away and very remote; he had climbed higher, trying to catch up with the dog. The roofs of the outbuildings were grassier than he remembered. The cattle huddled miserably against the barn walls. The sheep were lower, brought down to safety in the fields closest to the house. Andrew could hear them if there were a dog among them. Geordie did not think of the flooding of the upper pastures. He had never seen the mountainside after a really heavy storm.

The night had gone and it was dawn. Geordie must have slept. He looked down, to a rutted track, edged with grass, to the lurching poles of a wire fence, intended to repel the deer, though Geordie had seen stags wriggle through the wire strands and run on, ignoring the barrier. The few trees were landmarks. Above him, the bulk of the mountain was white from the hail that lay like snow in the gullies.

Beyond him, the burn was wild water, swelling over the fall, thundering downwards.

Geordie had to go down.

He would have to face Andrew's anger. If he stayed here, he would die. He was so cold. Hands and feet were numb and even his lips felt numb. He could not stop shivering.

He tracked downwards, as the sun blazed suddenly from a clearing sky. Steam rose from the flanks of the mountain, a mist haze that softened the harsh lines and momentarily hid the stark ground. It was barren ground, boulder and flint and intermittent scree, leading to the long gradual grassy slope to the village.

Chapter Twelve

The wind had died with the storm's ending.

The air was very still.

Geordie heard the sounds first; heard the now familiar but still heart-stopping panic bleating of a harried flock, somewhere very close. He did not know that men were already there, waiting, that the dog, racing through the heather, had been seen by a shepherd who gave the signal to Andrew's farm below, and it was phoned from farm to farm, when Tom saw the white cloth waving. From each farm came a man, silent, wary, stalking quietly, grim-faced, gun at the ready.

Geordie had travelled a considerable way down the mountain. He was crouched behind a dry-stone wall that separated Andrew's sheep from the moors beyond. The dog was working them, on the far side, away from him. There were men ranged all round the field. He could see them now. Men waiting to kill his dog, to take from him the last chance he had of rescuing the only creature that had ever been truly his.

He wanted to shout to them, to yell to them to stop, to scream and warn the dog, but if he did so the dog might pause to identify the direction of the sound and run straight into the path of the guns. If he kept quiet, perhaps the dog would sense danger, and run and vanish in the heather.

The dog had no eye for anything but the lamb it was herding.

He separated it swiftly from the flock, and chased it. It fled, terrified, straight towards Geordie, the dog at its heels, springing to its shoulder.

The guns spoke.

The dog somersaulted twice, and died.

Geordie ran towards it, his throat choked by an

enormous lump.

His dog!

He bent to take the body in his arms, and then he stared. Flash had been muddy, but this dog was clean. The white mark down the centre of the head was broader than that on Flash's head, and this dog had four black paws, and a white tip to his tail. Geordie let the body fall and, as Andrew and Tom reached him, he drummed frantically at Andrew's chest, shouting.

'It isn't Flash. It isn't Flash. It isn't Flash.'

Andrew examined the dog and bit back the words he was going to say. The boy was soaked and exhausted and shivering with shock and relief. This was no time for recriminations and anger, however well deserved. The farmer put his coat round the boy, and he and Tom made a fireman's chair and carried him back to the farmhouse.

Geordie couldn't stop shivering.

Andrew remembered his mountain lore. A sweet drink, not too hot. No sudden warming. No brandy. They wrapped Geordie in blankets and laid him on the bed and rang for the doctor. Tom sat by the bed, brooding.

The doctor diagnosed exposure. Geordie had to go to hospital. Andrew travelled in the ambulance, holding the boy's hand. Geordie was doped and half asleep, half demented, talking feverishly and rapidly of Flash.

'It wasn't Flash,' he said, catching Andrew's eyes, momentarily lucid.

'No. It wasn't Flash. It was the dog belonging to the young family at the edge of the Forestry Commission land. The wife goes to work and lets the dog out every morning before she goes; it goes home at night, and she never has the least idea what it's up to all day. You can't keep a sheepdog like that. It needs training and controlling. It had a rogue for a grandfather too, and bad blood will out. You have to take care when you buy a collie. Some of them are devils.'

The words were brief comfort.

'I want Flash,' Geordie said. 'He came . . . he licked me. Up on the hill. He's up on the hill. It's cold on the hill . . . It wasn't Jennie's fault. Jonathan wouldn't marry her with me there. I thought I'd best come. Then he'd come back. It wasn't the twins' fault. They wanted to tell.'

Andrew was beginning to glean a story he did not like. He waited until Geordie was comfortably in bed in the hospital and then took the train home and rang Angus who questioned the twins until Davina was in tears.

'You hopeless insane little nitwits,' their father shouted at them. 'How many times have I warned you about being alone on the mountain? How many times have I told you it's something no sane person ever does? How could you let Geordie go up there all alone? Why didn't you tell us?'

The twins didn't know. It had seemed a good idea at the time and they had been sure Geordie would come to no harm. He had food and shelter and it was good weather when he started out.

'The weather changes fast,' Angus said, despairing of the twins ever growing up and gaining sense. 'You know the story of the shepherd of Long Glen who died on a summer night in a storm like the one last night, swept away by the torrents. Geordie doesn't know the mountain well.'

'He followed the sheep paths. Sheep are always sensible about their trails,' Donald said, unwilling ever to admit himself in the wrong.

The twins were more concerned than they cared to admit when they went with Andrew to visit Geordie in hospital. His soaking in the storm had chilled him, and he was flushed and feverish, and desperately worried about Flash, still alone on the hill, wandering hungry and forlorn. And the doctors were anxious about his leg. He had strained the healing muscles badly on his journey and would limp worse than before, maybe for ever.

By now Jennie and Chas had arrived and were staying in the local hotel. They visited, neither knowing quite what to say. Geordie was far too ill to be scolded.

'He'll be OK,' Chas said that night, seated comfortably in Andrew's big kitchen. 'But the Lord knows what you're going to do with him. He'll never settle in a town.'

'It was madness to try,' Tom said irritably, not at all sure that Geordie would be all right. The mountains had killed older and stronger men and the lad had been out in the worst weather of the year, and chilled to the bone. He could have told all of them they were wrong before but no one ever asked for his opinion. He was only the hired help. Not his place to say, but this time his tongue got the better of him and he couldn't save it for Queenie. Tom was a direct man who frequently found the tactical manœuvres of cleverer people quite beyond his comprehension.

'We had no choice,' Andrew said. 'Jennie had the right; and she had to try, or she would never have forgiven herself.'

Jennie smiled at him gratefully. She was too relieved to know that Geordie was safe to have any regrets now. Chas had helped her. She had to accept that she had tried and she had failed. Now they had to find another solution.

'I'd like the boy to stay here,' Andrew said.

Tom, stroking one of the new kittens that was just beginning to tumble around the hearthrug, dug his fingers so hard into its fur that it bit him. He grinned at its miniature fury and soothed the soft fur until it purred again.

'Without a woman in the house?' Jennie asked.

'My sister's coming to live. Her husband has just died, and I've offered her a home,' Andrew said. 'We both wanted children and we both missed out. Not because we didn't try. My wife died too soon, and somehow no babies ever came for Kitty. The boy would be more than welcome here.'

176

'But what sort of future is there?' Jennie asked doubt-fully.

'He'd inherit the farm. I've no heirs,' Andrew said.

'But . . .' Jennie was at a loss for words. To her farming was a depressed industry. Living in the backwoods among animals seemed to her something only the unintelligent would do well at.

Chas was aware of her lack of understanding.

'Jennie's got the townee idea about farming,' he said. 'Look, Jennie, it's not the way you think at all. My family are farmers. Farmers need to be highly skilled these days. They need to know an enormous amount about stock keeping, about breeding, about genetics, or they get animals that have inherited faults, or cows that are poor milkers, or only have limited resistance to disease. They need to know how to get the best out of their land, whether they are using it for sheep, cattle, or crops. Need to know animal husbandry and animal psychology; to be as well able to recognise illness as any vet. My father can tell you exactly how many cows you can keep to the acre and what sort of land is best for them, can tell you to the minute when the calf is due to be born, and deliver it unless it's very tricky. You can't just shove a herd in a field and leave them there, you need extra feed in winter; you have to watch they don't get too much of the first new grass, or they become ill from that. Too many cattle in a field and the ground's ruined for grazing, and fouled. You need to know how to get the best milk yield, not only from which breed of cows, but from the individual cows. Get a harsh cattle man, and the cows won't yield nearly so much milk as they do with a good stockman. You need to know how to feed them to make good calves. Need to know how to foal a mare; how to drive and maintain a tractor; how to operate the silo and the milking parlour; how to shear a sheep in less time than it takes you to mark an exercise book; how to keep records, accounts, sort out VAT. It's no job for the thick witted, believe you me.'

Jennie stared at him.

'I never even thought about it,' she said.

'That's the trouble with townees,' Tom said bitterly. 'Just you come with me, miss, and I'll show you what farming's about.'

They went out.

'Tom'll blind her with science of his own, and talk a lot of nonsense,' Andrew said, but he did Tom an injustice. The man was incensed, and intended to show this girl from the Midlands just what sort of a farm they ran.

He showed her the milking parlour and the feed sheds and the silo; showed her the cattle and discussed the various breeds: Herefords and Ayrshires; Friesians and Jerseys; Guernseys and Charollais; Aberdeen Angus, Galloways, Shorthorns and Welsh Blacks. Jennie had never been aware that cows came in different shapes and sizes: that a Jersey was small and compact, yielding very rich milk, though she knew vaguely about goldtop and silvertop at the dairy. Friesians were very much larger; they yielded greater quantities of much less creamy milk.

But at least, Jennie said, sheep were sheep.

And found Tom reeling off names at her. Longwools; and the breeds of the various counties; Leicesters and Wensleydales; Teeswaters; Lincolns; Devon Longwools; Southdowns; Scottish Blackfaces; Cheviots; Black Welsh; Derbyshire Gritstones. Jennie was bemused. She had never even realised that there were different kinds of sheep.

She was more careful when she asked about pigs. The only breed that stuck in her mind was the Gloucester Old Spot. She knew there were different kinds of heavy horses. She came back amazed, her head reeling with all kinds of details. Even ducks it seemed were not just ducks. The two big drakes on the pool were Rouens.

She had discovered that lambing was late on the mountains, that many of the farmers used contract shearers who descended for a few days, sheared the whole flock and disappeared again. Tom thought nothing of that. He sheared his flock; and aimed to keep up a steady four minutes a sheep. Jennie learned about dipping as well.

'Still think farming's for dimwits?' Andrew asked, his eyes amused, as she came back into the room and Tom made tea and produced a rich cut and come again cake that the twins had brought with them the day before.

'Heavens no,' Jennie said. 'I had no idea. I'll be able to give a jolly good lesson on it when I get back to school.'

Geordie had only one thought in his mind when Andrew visited him in hospital. Jennie and Chas had already called, but it was useless talking to them.

'I've got to find Flash,' Geordie said.

Andrew was convinced that Flash must be dead of hunger long before now. He did not know what to say.

'He's out on the hills,' Geordie said. 'I saw him.'

'No, Geordie, you saw the other dog and mistook him for Flash. There's been bad weather. Flash can't have survived. He's not used to living wild,' Andrew said.

'Flash is there,' Geordie insisted. 'I saw him. He came and licked my hand. He knew me. Only he was scared of people and someone shouted and he ran away.'

'Geordie, lad, you dreamed it,' Andrew said patiently. No use raising false hopes. The dog had been missing for over a month. Unless he too were killing sheep . . . There had been enough killed to account for two dogs running wild.

'He wouldn't kill sheep,' Geordie said, almost as if he were able to thought-read.

Andrew was unsure. Suppose Flash had kept himself alive by eating the other dog's kills? There would be no embargo against taking flesh already dead. Suppose the dog had now acquired a taste for mutton? Suppose he were still out there, killing on his own account? But there had been no more reports of dead lambs since the killer died. His owners were furious, quite convinced the men

179

had made a mistake. The dog had shown no sign of his sins when he reached home late each evening.

Andrew did not like his thoughts.

'Please, as soon as I come back, can we look for Flash? Before I go back to Jennie?' Geordie had no illusions left. He had no choice. But he would like to know his dog was safe before he went. 'It's no use anyone else looking; he's got nervous and he'll only come to me. He went to look for me. He wasn't happy with the twins. He's my dog.'

'All right, we'll look,' Andrew promised. He knew there was no choice. For the boy's own sake, they would have to try. 'But don't set your heart on it. There's been wild weather on the hills and the dog may well have been swept away in the torrents. The other dog was much older, and he was weather wise. And he had a home to return to every night. He knew too much for his own good, that one.'

'Flash will know what to do,' Geordie said obstinately. Then he reverted to his other big worry. He hadn't intended to say anything, but he couldn't help himself. 'Have I got to go back with Jennie? Jonathan was angry with her because of me. I heard him shouting at her when I came home from school, so I didn't go in. I stayed outside, but he said he wouldn't marry her with me around. I couldn't help hearing. We had to have fried onions for supper.'

Boys, Andrew thought in despair. What on earth goes on in their heads? What have fried onions to do with anything?

'Why?' he asked at last, totally baffled, but sensing there was more to the statement than was at first evident.

'So I couldn't see Jennie had been crying,' Geordie said. 'But I could. Onions wouldn't have made her eyes so red so fast. Then I got Davina's letter about Flash, so I came home.'

Home. One little word. He had lost everybody and everything and he had lost his dog and they had sent him to live in a strange place among strangers. Andrew had a sudden unpleasant memory of a lamb he had found the year before, standing beside its dead mother. He had brought it down to hand-rear but it too had died. Died of grief, Tom had said, as much for the familiar circle of ground and the few shrubby bushes that were home, as for its dead dam.

He hadn't meant to say anything to Geordie yet. It was perhaps Jennie's place to tell him. Andrew didn't know. He didn't want the boy to feel that yet another person had rejected him. But Geordie was looking at him with desperation in his eyes, and now was the time; not later.

'Would you like to live with me, Geordie?' Andrew asked. 'I wanted to have you before, but Jennie *is* your family and she needed to try; she'd have never forgiven herself if she hadn't. It's no one's fault it didn't work. My sister's coming to live with me, as her husband died suddenly last week. She'd like to have you there too. We'd both have liked a son; but it never happened. And the farm can be yours when you grow up, if you want it. There's nobody else.'

Geordie said nothing, but the hand that gripped Andrew's so fiercely told the farmer all he wanted to know.

'We'll look for Flash, I promise,' Andrew said.

That night, Geordie lay awake savouring the thought of returning to the farm; remembering his room there; his own room now. He fell asleep and dreamed of a small collie coming towards him, legs half bent, tail half wagging, affection gleaming in the amber brown eyes.

By morning he was so improved that the doctor promised he could go home next day.

He savoured the thought. Now at last, home had some meaning. All he needed for perfection was Flash

Chapter Thirteen

Flash had learned a great deal while he was running free. He had learned to avoid the killer dog, which fought brutally, giving no quarter. He had learned about weather and wind; and he had learned a little about storms. But the storm on the hills was worse than anything he had ever endured in his short life and there was no one to reassure him. He could not understand the flashing lights in the sky; he could not understand the thunder rolls that echoed on the hills, the long slow peals continuing almost endlessly, without any pause between them.

Lightning cleft the sky. Lightning forked and hit the ground. Lightning flashed in continuous sheets.

He had never known such rain.

First came the hail, savaging his small body so that he crouched soaked and helpless, under the lee of a rock that gave little protection. He made himself small, his paws over his eyes, his frightened body shivering. He longed for someone to come and stroke him and soothe away fear.

High on the hill a tree was struck and it fell with a crack of sound that made the dog run, even with the rain beating against him, and creep into a hollow, his back to the wicked night.

The storm continued for hours, the flickering flashes opening the sky. They hurt the dog's eyes. Flash whimpered to himself, needing his mother; needing Geordie; needing home.

Then the water began to rise. The bed of the burn was of boulders, tumbled together. As the surging water pounded down the mountains, the boulders began to roll, echoing the thunder crash. The dog had to change his resting place, to get away from the noise that deafened him, running as panic mad as the sheep that had been driven by the killer.

The noises herded him relentlessly.

He fled, not noticing where he was running, racing in a wide circle that brought him back to the surging water, so that once again he fled through the driving rain, once coming close to the ruin where Geordie sheltered. But there was no chance of scent lying on the wet ground, or of the familiar smell being borne on the wind that flailed the hillside.

The dog crept into cover among thick shrubby bushes, digging at the ground to make a den for himself, and remained there till the storm was over. When the noise ceased, he slept, exhausted by the terror that had stayed with him the long wild night through.

He dried himself in the sunshine, and then made his way towards Andrew's farm. He had a long way to go as his roving terror had taken him high, in search of shelter.

He slipped on the wet ground, but plodded determinedly on, wanting shelter from the weather that had defeated him at last. He had never known such rain. In all the days he had been free, the rain had come and had gone again, but never with such force, or with such an accompaniment. Now fear of another storm was greater than his fear of man.

The storm had loosened a tree from the ground. The roots tore away, and with them came stones from the top of the scree. The dog had just reached the edge of the scree, lower down. Some of the stones hit him. The tree slipped downwards, taking part of the hill with it. The dog flattened himself under a rock, watching the land slide away beneath him. He learned all over again that nothing was safe or sure, not even the ground beneath his feet.

He crouched there for a long time, much too afraid to move.

At last he summoned his courage.

He crept cautiously, skirting the long gash of raw earth torn by the avalanche. Beyond it was a river bed, which he had known only when it was dry. There had been very little rain on the hills since he had run away. Now the bed was a seething torrent, roaring over the rocky ledges, the noise deafening. He began to climb high, away from the water. He was terrified of the driving surge, where once he had known only rocks.

He slipped.

The rain had made the ground so muddy that the dog could not regain his balance. He fell into the water, which took him, so that he hurtled downwards, helpless. He fell into a maelstrom of white surf. He was battered by the branches of trees, as he paddled frantically, trying to keep his head above the surface. The pool was edged by rock. A long spur projected from the cliff face. The dog managed to haul himself out, and dropped flat, panting.

The sun, blazing now from a clear sky, dried his fur.

But Flash was cut off. He was marooned on the rocky spit, penned against the wall of the cliff, and he dared not face the water again and try to swim back to freedom. The current was fierce. The roar of the water appalled him. He ran to and fro on the ledge, barking, but there was no one to hear, and his cries for help would not have been heard above the watery tumult. At last he curled up and slept a deep sleep of sheer exhaustion.

When he woke, he lapped at the water, and slept again. The will to live was weakening. He was injured, bruised, and had lost all hope. He could not leave his prison. He dared not risk the water.

He had very little strength left. He had not fed for two days.

He curled up in the shade, as far away from the water as he could get, and stared forlornly at the flood that had marooned him.

Flash had given up.

Chapter Fourteen

Neither Andrew nor Tom believed that Flash was still alive. They, and the men on the other farms too, were sure that there had been only one stray dog on the hill – the killer dog. Flash had almost certainly come to grief, almost as soon as he left Angus's home, probably under the wheels of a car.

It was impossible that so young a dog could survive alone on the mountain for more than a month. Even if he had been alive, the storm would have finished him. The mountain burns were in full spate, tumbling headlong towards the village, fed to fatness by the heavy rain, and the roar of water sounded in everyone's ears.

It was no use trying to convince Geordie.

He knew his dog was alive. He knew they would find Flash. He refused to consider the immense odds stacked against finding so small an animal on the mountain. Yet even he, as they set off the day that Chas and Jennie drove back to Manchester, was daunted by the towering slopes and the knowledge that the dog could be anywhere.

Jennie and Chas had wanted to reassure him, but looking up at the vast peaks, they realised it would be wrong. Jennie had said goodbye and had assured Geordie that all was well with her; that she did not blame him, neither for wanting to come back to such a beautiful place, nor for Jonathan's defection. That would have happened in any case. They were not right for one another.

She had met Kitty, who had arrived the night before. Andrew's sister was pleased to find she would have something to distract her from her own grief. Geordie had taken over his old room, had slipped back into the familiar routine, was delighted to belong somewhere again, and somewhere that he loved, but all his thoughts were set on finding his dog. He could think of nothing else. He could talk of nothing else, and Kitty who had heard both Tom's and Andrew's doubts, wondered what on earth they would do when the boy was at last convinced that his dog had died, if not before, then he must have died in the storm. Running water was everywhere. The mountain gushed white; falls sprang from every rockface; streams flooded and flowed into the fields. Many sheep had died. How could the dog survive?

Andrew did not want Geordie to go with them that day; he felt the boy needed far more rest, but Kitty recognised the pent-up tension and thought it would be better for Geordie if he tried to search. He barely ate, and his eyes never ceased to quarter the hillside as if he could pick out the tiny shape of his collie, running back to him.

His leg was still aching, but he was not going to admit to that. No one was going to keep him from the search. No one else would be successful. Geordie knew that Flash wanted him; that they belonged together and nothing could keep them apart.

He barely noticed Jennie and Chas when they drove away to return to their jobs.

He looked for omens as they left the farm.

There was one magpie in the field turning over the ground, hunting under stones. The black and white plumage glittered sleekly in the sunshine. June had come with a rush of flowering; the hills were marbled with colour. One for sorrow. There had to be another bird, somewhere. He scanned the hedge anxiously. He looked at the trees.

Andrew and Tom were striding ahead, Megan at heel. She turned back, not wishing her party to be broken up. She was as anxious to keep her humans together as to herd the sheep in a satisfying pattern. She barked at Geordie and the two men paused, knowing her need, waiting for the boy to catch up. Andrew was sure that a day on the hill would be too much for the boy so soon after his recent adventure; but there was no choice. The lad was fretting and they had to try.

Andrew eyed the distant peaks. There were miles to search and the dog was a tiny object in all that distance. If he were still alive, he could be anywhere. Also he might well be in such bad shape, that even if they did find him, he would die on them in the next few days. Whichever way it went, there was more heartbreak for Geordie. Andrew had offered Geordie another pup, the pick of the litter from an excellent working bitch on a neighbouring farm. But no other pups would do.

A second magpie flew across the field and joined its mate. Geordie drew a deep breath. She must have been on the nest and maybe there were young. Or would the young have flown? Geordie did not know. Tom saw the bird too. They had once been fairly rare, but now they were breeding everywhere and he had seen more of them about than ever before in his life, as there was a nest in a tree near the farm, as well as this nest, on the edge of the slopes.

Geordie only knew that he had his omen. One for sorrow. Two for joy. He caught up with Tom and Andrew, and Megan relaxed.

The climb was slower than Geordie wanted. His leg was dragging. Twice Andrew had to stop himself from commenting that it was time to rest and the boy should go back to the farm and let them search. He slowed his pace and exchanged glances with Tom, who turned his head and surprised an expression of pain on the boy's face. They ought to turn back.

Geordie had borrowed a pair of binoculars and was sweeping the hillside with them. Scree; and the raging waters of the little burn, now unbelievably swollen; the surging roar of water over the rocks; the sudden movement of a black and white animal that caught at his breath, but that proved to be a small blackfaced lamb, half hidden in heather, hunting for his mother, from whom he had become separated. His urgent bleats could not be ignored, and Geordie had to contain his impatience as Tom and Andrew climbed the little cliff face towards the small animal and brought him down, and sent Megan off to find the ewe. She came, *baaing* urgently, speeding in front of the dog, and nosed the lamb, who set to suck at once, his small tail frantic. On any other day Geordie would have stopped, amused, but he only had one wish in his head. Tom and Andrew thought he had dreamed Flash's visit, but he knew the dog had been real, alive, and had come to him and licked his hand.

He also had a new fear. The dog must be weak with hunger unless he too had been killing lambs. But no lambs had died in the last few days. The sheep had been unharmed since the killer died.

There was no time for talking.

There was only time to take a deep breath and nerve himself at every step, to hope that Tom and Andrew would not notice that his limp was growing worse, or hear the quick sudden suck of his breath as he stumbled on uneven ground and the aching muscles knotted in protest.

The two men were only too aware of the limp; and of the whiteness of the boy's face. They walked slowly and unhappily and at lunchtime Andrew forced a long halt on a grassy patch under the lee of a rock, out of the wind that was once more niggling through the grass.

Geordie barely ate. Kitty had made sandwiches and baked a cake and put up a flask of coffee. The drink was welcome, but the food was hard to chew. There had been no sight or sound of a dog anywhere all through that morning, and Geordie, looking at the vast area spread out before him, began to understand that this was no simple problem.

Andrew, looking bleakly at the slopes, saw gully and crevasse and precipice; saw the sheer sides where men had once quarried stone; saw the deceptive potholes that delved deep into the ground at the drinking places; saw the rusty-red fox lope out of cover, a young hare in his jaws. Saw death in a hundred forms and a hundred places. If the dog had met the fox . . . or met the killer, a powerful dog that would fight to the death . . .

The eagle was overhead, soaring on the airstreams. Geordie looked up as the bird's shadow fled over the ground. The old worry returned. Would an eagle take a dog? The dog might fight and would well prove an unhappy mouthful.

'We haven't a hope,' Andrew said, not wanting to say the words, but feeling he must somehow put a stop to the boy's hopes. The disappointment would be so much greater in the end.

'I'd know if Flash was dead,' Geordie said. 'God wouldn't let him die.'

Andrew refrained from answering. The ways of God had long been a total mystery to him and he wished he had a child's trust still. It would make life so much easier. His not to reason why.

'It's time to go on,' Geordie said, long before Andrew and Tom had finished their meal. He waited restlessly while they drank and put away the food, in the satchel, and tidied up the ground. He saw a deer bounding out of the wood, and Megan barked, but Geordie had little interest. He needed to search; he wanted to drag the bracken, to flatten the grass, to hunt through every shrubby thicket, through every bush. His dog might be lying there, ill, or injured, needing help, only a few yards from him and he might never know.

Clouds were gathering on the hillside. There would be more rain. The slopes were dark, the peaks hidden, and from far away came another thunder growl.

'You are not getting another wetting,' Andrew said. 'You're more important than any dog, lad, so it's home now. We'll come out tomorrow if the weather's fit. I'm not risking another chill.'

There was no chance to argue. Geordie knew when

Andrew spoke firmly there was no changing his mind.

He followed the two men forlornly, hating both of them for the moment. They didn't even try to understand. As if it mattered if he did get wet. Megan, off duty, ran endlessly to and fro, between Geordie, who was lagging, and the two men, chiding the boy for his slowness, barking at the men to wait, to let him catch up, to ensure all her people were together.

Flash had herded them too. Geordie wanted the dog so badly that he could not speak when he got in. Kitty, sure he was exhausted, was furious with her brother, and insisted on putting the boy to bed. He lay, not caring about anything, watching the distant peaks, willing himself to see a small black and white dog, his tail gay, trotting down the hillside, coming home.

That night thunder rumbled endlessly again and lightning flashed on the hills. Geordie thought of his dog, in the wet, alone, and could not sleep.

He fell asleep at last, exhausted, when the clouds parted and the sun rose and the birds greeted the morning. It was four o'clock, and light came early.

He woke at five-thirty at the clang of the milking churns, and was dressed and downstairs before Tom arrived.

'When are we going up the hill?' he asked Andrew.

Andrew and Kitty exchanged despairing glances.

'I'll have a word with Tom,' Andrew promised. It was all he could promise.

Geordie spent the next hour sitting on the wall, quartering the mountain with the binoculars. He saw sheep and running deer; he saw the plume of smoke from a distant cottage and saw the postman on his rounds. Nowhere was there a trace of a small black and white dog.

It was half term. The twins and Catherine McGregor came over to help. Catherine and the twins went up one side of the mountain and Geordie and Andrew took the other. Tom, who had many jobs to do around the farm, quartered the lower slopes with Megan, having left Kitty to take over some of his work. She was glad to have occupation. It left less time for memories.

'Find Flash,' Tom said, and Megan, mystified, trotted hopefully, tracking to and fro, and in circles; and then she hunted along a mazy path that led her to a lamb in trouble, a long twisting bramble stick caught in its woolly fleece under the tail, so that Tom had to spend time cutting away the wool to free the animal.

The rain had brought even more water down from the tops. Today there was a wind, a surge and a roar that made a constant background to their conversation.

Andrew hunted on, but he was hurt. He had thought Geordie would be overjoyed to find he was staying in Scotland, and that the offer of a home would make up to him for the loss of the dog. The farmer had not realised how much Flash meant to the lad.

Geordie was climbing more easily today. The rest had helped his leg, but pain still troubled him. He watched the ground carefully, so that he did not jar it suddenly on loose rock, or fall down a rabbit hole. His small face was set, his mouth determined, and Andrew became aware that Geordie had grown through several years in the short time that he had been away. He had learned a great deal very fast, and had learned he could rely on no one but himself. There was a new reserve, a wariness that had not been there before.

Andrew wished the boy would talk; his own thoughts were sorry company. He looked back. Catherine and the twins were some distance away, Davina hunting wholeheartedly through the bushes, still nagged by guilt, still sure that it was her fault entirely that the dog was lost. Donald was pretending to hunt, certain the dog was dead, and wishing he was elsewhere on his own affairs. Catherine had a pair of binoculars and was using them to scan the hillside, moving them purposefully, trying to cover every inch.

'The waterfall in the glen is three times its normal size,' Andrew said, wanting to distract the boy. 'Have ye ever seen it when the burn's in spate?'

Geordie shook his head. He was giving up. He knew now that Andrew had been right. The dog could not be alive. He had to reconcile himself to life without Flash.

'Geordie, I'll get you the best pup in the whole of Scotland,' Andrew said, hating to see the despair on the boy's face.

'I don't want another dog. Not ever,' Geordie said passionately.

The farmer sighed. He would never understand the boy as long as he lived. He did not realise that Geordie could not bear the thought of another dog living only a short while and then dying and leaving him behind to mourn all over again. He couldn't face it. He had had to face too much since his parents died and left him on his own.

'Come and see the falls,' Andrew said, anxious to distract the boy and not knowing how to continue the conversation. 'It's a once in a lifetime sight. That was one of the worst storms I've ever known in my life. I've only seen the falls once like this before and that was when I was about your own age.'

There was no point in hunting any further. It didn't matter whether he saw the falls or not. Geordie followed Andrew. Catherine and the twins joined them as they crossed the damp ground, spray blowing into their faces.

They watched the water hurling itself downwards, sunlight trapped in each drop. The noise was phenomenal, so that Tom, reaching them, had to take each one by the shoulder and point to the path, wanting them to come higher up and look down on the maelstrom in the pool.

They stared, awed, at the raging torrent. Geordie wanted to be alone. He left them, and climbed higher, finding himself on a small plateau. The water here ran over the edge of a steep, but low, cliff. Here was the pool he had bathed in, but it was quite unrecognisable. The water swirled and foamed and frothed. The little ledge where he had crawled to dry was partly submerged, but the long spit beyond it was dry except for spray, and bright with sunshine. The cliff cast a long shadow and in that shadow was something, lying. An animal that slowly lifted its head . . . a black and white head, with floppy half pricked ears.

Geordie forgot the pain in his leg and raced down the slope, hurrying so fast that he almost passed Andrew who reached out an arm to steady him.

It was no use talking. Andrew gave the boy a small shake to remind him to be more careful. A slip on the wet ground and he would fall downwards to instant death. Geordie had already turned and was dragging the farmer by the sleeve up the path beside the waterfall. The dog had moved and stood in the sunshine, wagging an uncertain tail, looking up at Geordie, having recognised his master.

But it was as impossible to reach him as it was to fly with the eagle.

Geordie looked at the water, and looked at Tom and Andrew. Tom shook his head.

'No way,' his mouth formed the words, which were only half audible above the din of the falls.

But they could drop food to the dog. Perhaps they could keep him alive till the water subsided, and rescue him then.

Tom walked across to the top of the little cliff. The water fell to one side. The dog was able to lie out of the spray which was flung in the opposite direction by the wind. If the wind changed he would be in the wet, but the sun had dried his coat and he had been lying in the shadow, out of the heat.

There were more than half the sandwiches left. The twins had some food left as well. Both Catherine and Kitty had made twice as much as was needed, knowing that appetites grew hearty, walking on the hills. If they could drop the food to the dog he could feed. He was pitifully thin. He was clean now, washed by the water. If only the parcel of food would fall true, and not drop into the falls.

Tom had a large neckerchief tucked into the collar of his shirt. He took it off and put the food inside, leaving a wide gap, and weighted the bundle with a stone. He dropped it over. It fell within yards of the dog, who stared at the unlikely object with fear. Flash dropped to the ground again, sure that once more men had let him down and thrown something at him, meant to hurt. He lay with his nose on his paws, disconsolate.

Geordie was praying harder than he had ever prayed in his life. Praying that the dog wouldn't jump in the water and try to reach them. Praying that Flash would get up and look at the parcel and smell the food. Stupid dog. Idiot dog. Good dog, look at it then, go and find it . . . Geordie willed the words down to the dog below him with such fervour that he was not in the least surprised when Flash crawled uncertainly towards the bundle, having caught a whiff of food-smell on the wind, and sniffed at it.

A moment later the dog had his front paw on the cloth to hold the package steady, was ripping it open, was savaging the food. He ate every crumb.

'We can go and get more,' Geordie yelled to Andrew above the roar of the water.

Andrew nodded. He was eyeing the cliff face. If this amount of water was anything like that which had flooded over in his own youth, it would be days before it was low enough to rescue Flash; and the dog was constantly at risk as he might become so lonely that he would attempt to swim the falls and he would most certainly drown.

There was a faint possibility . . . if they could call in the mountain rescue team; he knew the men and was sure they would help so long as there was not a more pressing emergency on the hills. There were so many accidents in high summer. He did not want to raise Geordie's hopes too high and there was nothing whatever to be done that day. It was already almost milking time, and he wasn't leaving the boy on the mountain alone, lest his longing for the dog overcame all sense of caution and he drowned trying to rescue the animal.

Flash had finished the food. He sat, watching the faces above him, now knowing they had helped him and expecting to be rescued from his predicament. Andrew touched Geordie on the shoulder and pointed down the mountain. Reluctantly Geordie followed the rest of the party. If only he could make Flash understand that they were coming back.

The dog watched them go. His pricked ears dropped, his tail went down between his legs and he whined, high and thin, forlorn. The sound was lost amid the roar of the water. Geordie looked back. He wanted to stay but he knew he could do nothing. The dog walked slowly back to his former position against the cliff, out of range of the spray, and curled up, nose to tail. He got up again and walked across to the paper and torn up rags, nosing it, licking at the last traces of crumbs. There was nothing left to eat but at least he now had food inside him. He drank from a pool that had collected on the rock, and slept again.

Geordie, helping with the milking, thought of his dog alone on the rock. He could think of nothing else and twice Tom had to chide him sharply for standing doing nothing when there was work to finish.

'There's nothing at all we can do tonight,' Andrew said, knowing Geordie's thoughts. His own were on similar lines. It would be terrible to find the dog, only to lose him again before they got him to safety. 'I'll ask the mountain rescue team to help, but they can't get here quickly; they can't work at night either. I'll do all I can, I promise you.'

Geordie helped Kitty lay the table. She was very like

her brother, slim and dark, though there were grey hairs among the black. Andrew's hair was not yet touched by time. She moved quickly, with birdlike gestures, and was deft and neat and competent.

'No one can work miracles, Geordie,' she said, piling the table high with food, as the twins and Catherine were staying to tea. Tom had decided that Kitty was an asset; they had never fed so well on their own; she was a cook in a thousand. Catherine watched the twins eat and wished Geordie would eat too. He crumbled his bread, and played with the home-cured ham and the salad, and ignored Kitty's splendid cakes, his thoughts on the mountain where a small black and white dog faced yet another night alone, trapped, and in extreme danger.

Chapter Fifteen

Three men arrived at dawn next morning in the mountain rescue team's Land-Rover. Andrew knew one of them, John Timmis, a big, bearded, merry man who was happier on rock faces than at ground level. He was an instructor at the Aviemore sports centre, teaching climbing and skiing. He added to his income by writing articles on mountaineering and was busy with his first book. His Alsatian bitch, Nikki, was well known to everyone around as she had tracked and found a number of lost walkers, and also found people buried in snow avalanches. Her nose was invaluable on the hills. She had no part to play today, but she was never far away from John and she often guarded the equipment in the Land-Rover. She sat beside John now, in the front passenger seat, and Geordie, looking at her, wished that Flash were also safe.

He was desperately worried in case they refused to risk their lives rescuing a dog, as John would not commit himself. He wanted to see the place first before he made up his mind. If it were too dangerous, they could not risk human lives. The big man looked at Geordie, and, quick to sense other people's worries, smiled as he whistled to his bitch.

'I'd go to hell and back for Nikki,' he said. 'I know how you feel, lad. I promise we'll do our best and if there's a chance for your dog we'll take it. We're all used to tricky places and it might not be so bad as you think.'

They drove the Land-Rover as far as possible up the hillside, and then left it and walked. John talked all the time, telling Geordie of mountain rescues in gales and storms, of helicopters hovering close to cliff faces, of men marooned on sheer rock, or trapped on narrow ledges, sometimes through bad luck; more often through bad judgement. Few people realised how swiftly the weather changed on the high peaks, or how even on a basking hot day down below, the wind on the tops was bitterly cold and could bring snow and ice in its wake.

Geordie's leg hurt less today and it was easier to keep up. Also this time he had hope to buoy him, although he had one thought he dared not face. He pushed it away as soon as it came. All the same the worry needled. Suppose the water had risen in the night and swept the dog over the falls?

Kitty had made a doggy pack, of the remains of a joint, and of dog biscuits, and padded it thickly with paper that the dog could tear away. She soaked part of it in gravy to attract him. Flash loved gravy with onions and Geordie had told Kitty how they had to punish him for stealing it on occasions. Andrew did not want too much food in the pack; the dog had been eating little and it might upset him to give him more than he could take. They would have to build him up slowly. Geordie clutched the parcel as if it were a life line and plodded on, unaware of the brilliant sky and the vivid colours around him. The June weather was holding.

'No fear of storm today,' John said as they climbed over the shoulder of the hill, turning away from the slope that led back to the village, coming on to much steeper ground. The noise of the falls was in their ears. As they topped the first small peak the full fury of the water met them. Geordie looked at it with a sinking heart. Surely there was more water than ever?

'Where is the dog?' asked the second of the mountaineers, Dannie, a tall fair student from Glasgow University who had just finished his exams and had joined the team for the rest of his long vacation. His blond hair was almost waist length, his blouse and jeans were pale blue, embroidered with flowers. He wore a gold pendant round his neck, but Geordie soon found he was as tough as John, climbing tirelessly, always ahead of them, dropping back at intervals to talk to Geordie and cheer him up, teasing him as he teased his own small brother, vivid memories of his own childhood not so long behind him.

The last member of the party, Sam, was much older than the others, a small man with grey hair and intense blue eyes and little conversation, but he turned often with a warm smile that helped Geordie as much as the teasing and the talk from the other two.

Tom had stayed behind to help Kitty, who had taken up the life of a farm wife as if she had never left it. She had lived at the edge of a town, without animals, and had missed them. It was good to be back among them. She worked on, her thoughts with the party on the mountain, knowing that rescuing the dog would do more to help Geordie than anything that she or Andrew could do.

Andrew walked beside Geordie, ready to help him if necessary, but careful not to offer help unless it were essential. He knew Geordie hated any reference to his lame leg. But there was no doubt the gruelling days on the mountain had made the limp much worse. They'd have to get the doctor to have a look and perhaps start another course of physiotherapy again. Once the dog was safe.

They reached the plateau and looked down over the ledge towards the spur beyond the water where Flash had been trapped. The light was fierce, the sun hot on the rock, and the shadows were black. At first Geordie thought the dog had gone. There was no sign of him anywhere.

Andrew also thought the dog had been swept away, and then, with a sigh of relief, he pointed.

The dog was lying in the deepest shade, out of reach of the baking heat of the sun. He could not hear the men above him. He slept, curled nose to tail, almost all the white hidden, so that he merged with the shadows.

Geordie dropped his parcel on the ledge.

The dog's ears pricked.

He looked up and wagged his tail. His mouth opened and Geordie knew that Flash was barking, but they could hear only the din of the water pouring endlessly over the rocks.

The parcel had dropped against the cliff face, well away from the water. The dog went to it, tore away the paper and began to eat.

'He's fit enough,' John said. He had locked the Land-Rover and brought Nikki with him so that she could lie in the shade. It would be far too hot in the car. She lay under a tree, nose on paws, knowing she must not move. Her head turned to watch John, never losing sight of him, waiting hopefully for a signal to call her to him. Andrew had left Megan with Tom, who had to look over the sheep. They did not like leaving them unshepherded too long. There was always something . . . a sheep caught in wire, a lamb trapped on a ledge, or separated from its mother; a foot festering because of a thorn. Leave the sheep too long without supervision and there might be bad trouble, not slight trouble. A dead lamb, or a hoof injury turned gangrenous.

John and Dannie had gone higher up the hill to survey the ledges and to discuss their procedure. Andrew lay on the grass looking down at the dog. It was in pretty good shape considering the length of time it had been running wild. There were obvious injuries, but they could soon be put right. The water had cleaned the dog, but he was starvation thin, as was only to be expected. Since seeing Geordie, Flash had begun to want to live again. His time on the hills had toughened him. He waited patiently for rescue, now needing men, and aware that these men had come to help him. He finished eating and settled himself at the edge of the shade, watching Geordie. The amber brown eyes never faltered. He might have been setting a sheep; the unwavering stare continued, the dog never turning his head, his mouth open, tongue lolling out, in a half laugh. Megan worked the sheep with the same intense gaze.

John came down the slope again, scrambling over the rocks, moving effortlessly.

He had to cup his hands round his mouth and shout at the top of his voice to make himself heard.

'The cliff face isn't too bad, it looks worse than it is. If we rope Geordie would he like to go down and rescue his dog? There's more chance that Flash will trust him than one of us. There's a small cliff above we can practise on; Geordie only needs to balance himself against the face of the rock on the way down and to use his feet on the way up. The dog doesn't look heavy.'

Geordie's face was alight with eagerness. He could do something at last, and he would rescue his own dog. No one else. He looked down at the cliff face and at the seething water, at the falls beyond, and then wished he hadn't. But he followed John up the slope and stood while the ropes were settled safely about him, and watched as Dannie demonstrated the way he needed to lower himself, helping to take his own weight, instead of being a dead weight on the rope.

It looked simple enough on the little cliff face, with grass beneath him. He knew it would not be so simple on the steeper cliff above the water, with the noise in his ears, and the dog in his arms. Suppose he dropped Flash? Suppose the rock came away from the cliff? Suppose the rope broke? Geordie had a vivid imagination and he had never even wanted to climb before.

Andrew cupped his hands and bellowed. His voice was softer than John's and it was a strain to make himself heard.

'Are you sure you want to go? I'll go down if you like. The dog knows me.'

There was no chance. Geordie shook his head vigorously. He wanted to go. He wanted to start, now.

'No hurry,' John shouted. Impatience was dangerous.

'Take it slow and easy or we'll all be in trouble. Do exactly as I told you, and it will be as safe as crossing the road.'

Geordie nodded.

His heart was beating wildly and he was afraid, but he was more afraid for his dog than for himself. He lowered himself very gently over the lip of the cliff, feeling the rope tighten as Dannie and John and Sam and Andrew gripped it. John had spread his anorak over the cliff edge to stop the rope from rubbing. It was not far down. Only twenty feet, no higher than a house. There were stunted trees at the edges of what looked, from his new position, to be a narrow gorge.

He concentrated on the trees, rooted there in the rock, leaning towards him, almost leafless, growing at the edge of the rapids. He wondered how they anchored themselves, wondered if the roots would tear away if he grabbed them by accident, and then he looked up, as he swung suddenly and terrifyingly, away from the cliff, above the spur, and had visions of himself crashing down as the ropes around him gave way, or the knots came undone.

He remembered what he had been told and grabbed at the cliff.

He knew he would have to dangle helplessly, like a spider, spinning on the end of a thread, when he had Flash in his arms.

The rock was rough and there were finger holds and toe holds. He could ease his lowering and he moved carefully, knowing that nothing he had ever done before was quite so dangerous, but that in spite of his fears, he was perfectly safe as long as he kept his head. The chief danger would be in coming up again.

His foot slipped and he caught his breath. The sudden jar hurt his leg, and he clung for a moment spread-eagled against the rock, feeling sick. The pain was getting worse. It was now a constant ache that took away some of his anxieties about the cliff, and added to his worry that he would never walk again without the telltale limp that dogged him now.

Even so, he could still do things like other boys. None of the boys he knew had ever climbed down above a waterfall with spray across his face. He looked up and John put his hand up, thumb uppermost, and smiled. Dannie signalled with his arm.

Easy. Easy. The slow movements told Geordie to take care.

Geordie concentrated on hands and feet.

The rock was slimed and green in places and his fingers failed to grip and his toes slipped. He moved delicately from crack to crack, once shaking with fear as a stone dislodged itself under his foot. Suppose it fell on Flash?

And then he was almost down and the dog was beneath him, jumping excitedly at him, trying to reach him, so that he was afraid of falling and landing on top of the collie. He eased himself to the ground. The spit was much bigger than he had realised, and on this side it was quite dry. The water made him dizzy, flinging itself in perpetual movement into the boiling pool.

Flash was leaping up at him, licking face and hands, obviously whining and barking, but there wasn't a sound to be heard. Only the thunder of the falls. Geordie knelt and the dog came to his arms, and wriggled in ecstacy, circling against the boy, trying to get close. He was thin and hurt, but he was alive and obviously far from dying. Geordie opened his anorak and zipped the dog inside, only his head projecting, just beneath the boy's chin. The lower part of the anorak was firmly bound by the rope. Flash would be quite safe.

Geordie could feel the dog's heart beating; could feel the warm breath on his face; could feel a consuming excitement that buoyed him to face the dizzy spinning against the rock, to fend himself off with his hands so that he and the dog didn't bang against the cliff, to swallow the sickness that suddenly overcame him as he unwisely looked down into the seething water, down to the plunging scree, down to great tumbled boulders that would kill him at once if he fell on them. He used his feet as Dannie had shown him. He used one hand to fend off the cliff. The other protected his dog. He had to make quite sure that Flash was safe.

He was at the top.

There were eight hands pulling him to safety.

There were Dannie and John and Sam and Andrew grinning with relief.

There was Nikki who had sensed the excitement and been unable to stay where she had been told, coming towards them, body weaving, tail waving, ears flat on her head, a grin on her face, as she knew that their efforts had been successful and that everyone was delighted.

Dannie offered to take Flash but Geordie would not let the dog go.

He held him tightly, avoiding the licking tongue that dirtied his face. He was covered in dust from the blown grit from the scree. He was soaked by the spray. His eyes gleamed with achievement.

John whistled to Nikki and they made their way down the hill. Geordie forgot the pain in his leg. He limped, but it was no longer important. Twice he almost tripped, unable to take his eyes off Flash and watch where he was going.

The twins were waiting at the farmhouse, and Angus was there, ready to examine the dog, and to marvel at him. His injuries were healing. He had obviously had a tough time, out there on the hills. Geordie bathed the wounds, and took the dog indoors.

Flash recognised the house.

He was home.

He left Geordie and raced round the rooms, greyhound fashion, leaping on and off Geordie's bed, so pleased to be back that he could not control himself. The men laughed as the dog whirled through each room, tore up the stairs, bounded down again, and leaped at Geordie, his tail threatening to come off. Each time he saw the boy he groaned with pleasure, and at last, completely exhausted, he fell asleep, curled against his master who had stretched out on the hearthrug. Geordie was so worn out with worry that he fell asleep himself, his arm around the dog, not wanting, ever, to be parted from him again.

By the time Geordie woke, Kitty had prepared a celebration tea.

But there was something that Tom wanted to know.

'There's facts to face, lad,' he said to Geordie. 'No use blinding yourself. That dog's been running wild and sheep have been killed. They may have kept him alive. He may have got a taste for mutton. We'll take him out in the field . . . and we'll watch. One go at those lambs, and what then?'

Geordie had thought it was over.

He wanted to cry.

He looked at Andrew, who nodded.

'We have to know. We can't keep a killer, Geordie. You know that.'

Silently, they went outside.

The dog followed them, jumping up eagerly at Geordie's hand.

He was home, he was safe, he had his master again.

Geordie dared not think. He knew that sheep had been killed and he had wondered uneasily if perhaps Flash had helped, but he had resolutely pushed the thought away, hoping it would not occur to Andrew or to Tom.

Tom opened the field gate.

It was only then that Geordie realised the man was carrying his gun.

'Best to get it over quick, lad, if we have to,' Tom said. No use glossing facts. The boy had to learn, just as the little devil with the cigarette, smoking in the hay, had had to learn. Geordie would have to find out there was no room for softness if he was going to be a farmer and that seemed to be the general idea.

Flash saw the sheep.

Instinct took over.

He forgot Geordie.

He forgot his injured paw, and forgot his bruises and bites and cuts. He began to herd. Slowly, gently, round the sheep. Geordie could not stand still and watch. He whistled, softly, remembering how he had taught Flash to work in the early days. The dog obeyed him at once, dropping at the signal. Now Geordie forgot everything; forgot Tom; forgot the dog might kill. They were alone on the hill, he and his dog, working the sheep. He signalled again and again. The dog ran left, ran right, brought in a straggler, and at the end singled one of the lambs. Geordie whistled again.

The dog dropped, tail beating against the ground.

Geordie called.

'Flashie boy, here. Good dog.'

The small body hurtled into his arms.

Geordie turned to face the house, where John and Dannie and Sam had returned for tea. Kitty had put on an impromptu party.

The farmhouse was full of laughter for the first time for months. Andrew, stretched out in the armchair, eating his food from a plate on his lap, too lazy to sit at table, watched as Geordie limped into the room and put the dog down on the hearthrug. The dog did not stay. He followed Geordie to the table, both limping.

'You're both laglegs,' Donald said, his mouth full of food. Davina kicked him under the table and he stared at her. 'Come on and eat, Geordie,' he added, suddenly guessing the reason for the kick, and embarrassed.

Davina had noticed the expression on Geordie's face and realised that lagleg was an expression he must hate. But as Geordie watched the dog limp towards his own plate, that

Kitty had just put down on the floor for him, he no longer cared. So what if they did limp? They could both get by. Flash could still herd sheep; and he could do everything that he could do before except perhaps play soccer well; and that wasn't such a great loss.

He looked out of the window at the towering peaks.

He had conquered the mountain and so had Flash. He turned his head as Tom broke the gun and showed it to him. It had never been loaded.

'He had to learn and I had to know,' he said to no one in particular.

'You're as big a fool as the boy is over that dog,' Andrew said.

Geordie said nothing. He did not think he felt like eating. He sat and watched the dog feed, and then, when Flash had finished and came to sit with his head on his master's knee, brown yellow eyes watching, intent, Geordie sighed deeply, and a moment later realised, as the smell of food wafted towards him, that he had never been so hungry in his life.

Tom had gone outside to talk to Queenie.

'He'll do,' he told the sow and scratched her ear.

She groaned in delight.